Anne I Robertson

Yaxley and Its Neighbourhood

A novel in three volumes. Part 3

Anne I Robertson

Yaxley and Its Neighbourhood
A novel in three volumes. Part 3

ISBN/EAN: 9783337045722

Printed in Europe, USA, Canada, Australia, Japan

Cover: Foto ©Andreas Hilbeck / pixelio.de

More available books at **www.hansebooks.com**

In 1 vol. Price 12s.

ON CHANGE OF CLIMATE,

A GUIDE FOR TRAVELLERS IN PURSUIT OF HEALTH.

By THOMAS MORE MADDEN, M.D., M.R.C.S. Eng.

Illustrative of the Advantages of the various localities resorted to by Invalids, for the cure or alleviation of chronic diseases, especially consumption. With Observations on Climate, and its Influence on Health and Disease, the result of extensive personal experience of many Southern Climes.

SPAIN, PORTUGAL, ALGERIA, MOROCCO, FRANCE, ITALY, THE MEDITERRANEAN ISLANDS, EGYPT, &c.

" Dr. Madden has been to most of the places he describes, and his book contains the advantage of a guide, with the personal experience of a traveller. To persons who have determined that they ought to have change of climate, we can recommend Dr. Madden as a guide.— *Athenæum.*"

" It contains much valuable information respecting various favorite places of resort, and is evidently the work of a well-informed physician, —*Lancet.*"

" Dr. Madden's book deserves confidence—a most accurate and excellent work."—*Dublin Medical Review.*

" It cannot but be of much service to such persons as propose leaving home in search of recreation, or a more benign atmosphere. The Doctor's observations relate to the favourite haunts of English invalids. He criticises each place *seriatim* in every point of view."—*Reader.*

" We strongly advise all those who are going abroad for health's sake to provide themselves with this book. They will find the author in these pages an agreeable gossiping companion as well as a professional adviser, who anticipates most of their difficulties."—*Dublin Evening Mail.*

" To the medical profession this book will be invaluable, and to those in ill-health it will be even more desirable, for it will be found not merely a guide for change of climate, but a most interesting volume of travel."—*Globe.*

" Dr. Madden is better qualified to give an opinion as to the salubrity of the places most frequented by invalids than the majority of writers on the subject."— *Liverpool Albion.*

" There is something, and a great deal too, for almost every reader in this volume, for the physician, for the invalid, for the historian, for the antiquarian, and for the man of letters. Dr. Madden has rendered a necessary service to the profession and to the public upon the subject under notice."—*Dublin Evening Post.*

" Dr. Madden's work is fraught with instruction that must prove useful both to practitioners and patients who study it."—*Saunders' News Letter.*

" Dr. Madden deserves the thanks of all those persons afflicted with that dire disease, consumption—as well as of those who suffer from chronic bronchitis, asthma, &c. It is the best work on change of climate that has ever been presented to the public."—*Daily Post.*

YAXLEY AND ITS NEIGHBOURHOOD.

A NOVEL.

IN THREE VOLUMES.

BY

The Author of "Myself and my Relatives," &c.

"How readily we wish time spent revoked,
That we might try the ground again where once
Through inexperience (as we now perceive)
We missed that happiness we might have found!"

COWPER.

VOL. III.

London:

T. CAUTLEY NEWBY, PUBLISHER,

30, WELBECK STREET, CAVENDISH SQUARE,

1865.

[THE RIGHT OF TRANSLATION IS RESERVED.]

YAXLEY & ITS NEIGHBOURHOOD.

CHAPTER I.

LONEHILL.

How she got up the steps, and into the house that first night, Lizette could never afterwards distinctly recall to mind; but she had a shadowy remembrance of having gone through a long narrow hall, very dimly lighted by a tallow candle, borne by an untidy-looking servant-woman, and having at last reached a very ill-furnished sitting-room, where a homely repast

was laid out upon a square oak table, covered by
a coarse, soiled tablecloth. There was a small
fire shedding out a faint glow of heat; for
although the grate was large enough, it was
packed at each end, to a considerable extent, with
red bricks, leaving only a little space in the centre
for coals. One large tallow candle standing
crookedly in a tall brass candlestick, was placed
in the middle of the table, dimly lighting up an
apartment of considerable size and general lugu-
briousness of aspect. The dark paper on the
walls was streaked and worn away in many spots
by damp and occasional downpours of rain through
the ceiling; the chairs were very black-looking
indeed, and upon close examination the antique
wood of which some of them were formed proved
to be dotted all over with tiny round holes, caused
by the fretting of mysterious insects. The carpet,
if ever it had boasted of any particular or defined
pattern or brilliancy of hue, had none certainly

now, though carefully protected from feet and
sunshine in many places by strips of linen,
which undoubtedly gave evidence, by its soiled
aspect, of how much dirt it saved its charge
beneath from ; there was no rug, but a piece of
the aforesaid dirty grey linen was spread over the
hearth where a rug should have been. Some
pictures in oil colours, all extremely sombre-
looking, and plentifully hung with a tapestry of
cobwebs, adorned the walls ; and lastly, two black
cats with gleaming eyes sat before the dim fire,
suggesting ideas of evil spirits and dark witchcraft. The mistress of the house was tall, strongly
formed, and upwards of seventy years old; she
wore a rusty black crape cap of pyramidal shape,
terminating in a peak at top, crowned by a bow
with floating ends, which suggested the idea of
a portentous flag flying from some high, lugu-
brious fortress ; her general attire was dark, if
not actually black—these sombre hues being

adopted for the purpose of disguising the unwashed
state of her garments; for there were two things
which Mrs. Bromley had a particular horror of
purchasing—these were soap and salt. Whether
she had ever been handsome her grandniece could
not of course determine; but she assuredly bore
now no trace of past beauty; her features were
strong and masculine, and her complexion rough
and bronzed; yet sometimes a pleasant glow
lighted up her countenance when she gave way to
one of her loud hearty laughs that sounded more
like the laughter of a man than of a woman. To
Lizette's surprise Simon Peggs was desired to
stay to supper, and he also became a partaker of
the homely meal o'erspreading the oaken board;
yet, although her grandaunt chose to sit at the
table with him, and talk familiarly to him, she
nevertheless maintained an air of much hauteur,
which always had the effect of keeping Mr. Peggs
in a state of extreme humility and respect, so

that he sat uneasily on the end of his chair and hardly seemed to understand correctly whether his tea was intended for his mouth or the floor. Mrs. Bromley had a somewhat original manner of helping her guests to the good things on the table, which rather surprised Miss Stutzer, who had never seen a precedent for it. The fowl, for instance, being very tough, she first nicked the joints with her own knife—for there were neither carving knives nor forks on the table—and then proceeded to twitch the limbs of the bird off with her dexterous fingers, placing a leg or a wing on the plate of either guest as they desired. On demanding in a loud tone, " Peggs, will you take some of this excellent fricassee which I made with my own hands ?" and, having received a most humble and reverent " Thank you, ma'am, I'll try it, please you," as answer to the question, she put a large iron spoon into the fricassee-dish, conveying therewith a very substantial mouthful to her own mouth, probably for the purpose of ascertaining if the fricassee really was as good as she had previously imagined it to be, and then smacking her lips, and, mumuring "delicious " in a *sotto voce,* musing tone, she again thrust the iron spoon into the dish, and, with dignified satisfaction, helped Simon to a considerable quantity of the well-seasoned compound.

"What are you about, Niece?" she asked, with the hearty manner of a jovial old gentleman, as she turned to Lizette, who was making but slow way with the viands given to her.

"Why are you not enjoying yourself more?"

Lizette assured her she was doing very well; but being fatigued, had not much appetite.

"Humph! why you must be very easily knocked up. I have travelled for three days and three nights often without closing an eye, and never felt even weary; and yet I don't suppose that I am a remarkably strong woman either.

Peggs, I don't remember ever feeling tired in my life."

"I am sure you don't, ma'am; sure you never were. You're a wonderful fine, active lady!" said Simon, looking reverently at Mrs. Bromley.

"Wonderful! Oh, no; but I never in my life gave way to affectation and conceited airs. My niece will soon learn to take pattern by my behaviour and energy."

Pegg was not quite convinced of this, as appeared by the doubtful look he cast upon the fragile, insignificantly-sized young lady, who seemed like a creature of another species beside her large grandaunt; but he held his peace. Towards the close of the evening an argument arose between him and Mrs. Bromley, touching a political question of the day—for Simon was a great politician, and in this respect would not concede to any one's opinion. He was conscientious, and he would not say what he did not think

to please either the Queen of England or Mrs.
Bromley; and thus a terrible outburst, on the
part of the latter lady, ensued. Miss Stutzer was
terrified; her grandaunt's face grew deep red, her
eyes flamed furiously, and at last she ordered
Peggs to leave the room—the house—the premises
—instantly, and never dare to come into her
presence again. The man got up as commanded
and made his exit with all speed, while Lizette
sat trembling and shocked at the table. She soon
saw, however, that Mrs. Bromley was by no means
deeply affected by her sudden outburst of rage;
it all passed off in a few minutes, and she coolly
began to talk to her of her journey and other
matters.

"There is a picture of your mother," she said,
pointing to a shadowy-looking portrait hanging
on the wall near the fireplace.

Lizette got up to examine it, and, as it was high
upon the wall, she stepped upon a chair that stood

near, in order to obtain a better view of it. A great shout proceeded from her grandaunt; but it was too late. Lizette was already in a perilous position. In a second she felt herself going through the bottom of the chair, which soon lay all at once broken—a wreck—on the floor. It was all a matter of chance whether her grandaunt fell into a rage or a fit of laughter; fortunately for her niece the merry mood prevailed, and Lizette was lifted from the ground with great good humour. Probably Mrs. Bromley never got into more than one passion per hour; yet she lamented the destruction of her handsome mahogany chair, which she said was not at all old, her father having purchased the set soon after his marriage and given a large sum for them. There were twelve of them originally, she said, but in some unaccountable way there were only three or four remaining. When Lizette was recovered from her alarm she ventured to ask her grandaunt about her old friend Peggy Wolfe.

" Oh, she stayed with me for a little while," said Mrs. Bromley, " but I turned her off at the end of a week. She was recommended to me as a servant by a woman at Clicksthorp; but she turned out one of the most dreadful creatures that ever came under my roof."

" Indeed! I am for sorry that. I used to think her an excellent woman."

" Excellent! She was lazy and impertinent— quite set above herself—wanting to have her own way in everything—cleaning the rooms every day, or reading religious tracts; and actually asking leave to go to church on Sundays! In every way she was unfit for a servant. I have no idea of servants going to church. Religion may be all very well in its way; but when it comes to servants wanting to go to church every Sunday, it's rather too much of a good thing!"

"But do you not think it makes them honest and faithful to be pious?" murmured Lizette.

"Honest and faithful! Never! never!—not a bit of it!" exclaimed Mrs. Bromley in loud emphatic tones. "I hate religious servants; I hate religious people altogether. The banker that robbed me was one of your religious tract-giving men; and the saddler at Clicksthorp, who ran away the other day, leaving all his debts unpaid, and ruining many people, was a canting, ranting Methodist. Don't talk to me of religion and piety!"

"But you speak of hypocrites, aunt," said Lizette gently. "Those two men whom you speak of could not have been really religious; they assumed the cloak as a disguise."

"Well, I don't care if they did. How am I to know whether it is a diguise or not? Am I to be a witch to know who the really religious people are, or who are hypocrites, and who true

Christians ? I keep clear of the whole thing ; that's my way. I don't want any religious people, in disguise or out of it, in my house."

" But, my dear aunt, you might as well say, you would never let a real gentleman into your house, because a well-dressed pickpocket had robbed you."

" Eh? What do you mean? Yes, they are all pickpockets, indeed. Religion is just a cloak for knavery and cheating and sneaking. I never liked pious people in my life ; that was one reason why I quarrelled with Paul Stutzer, your father. He wanted to turn my house upside down with his absurd notions. It always seemed to me that religious people were fault-finding, domineering, upsetting creatures, dictating to every one, and thinking no one as good as themselves. I never knew one of them that had a spark of real good-nature or feeling. It is all ' Put your trust in the Lord' on the tips of their tongues, while they are putting their hands into your pockets to rob you. I told that to the Vicar the other day when he called here to ask for a subscription to some charity, and I don't think he will trouble me for any money in a hurry again."

Poor Lizette looked at, and listened to her grandaunt in silence; a dark gloom seemed to steal over her soul; and yet Mrs. Bromley did not seem altogether unkind ; she was attentive, and anxious that she should make herself comfortable ; but her views on many subjects were overshadowed by great darkness.   She talked that evening often of Lizette's parents, and did not conceal her dislike of " Paul Stutzer," as she always termed her father.   The young girl knew enough of her temper to understand that she must not dare to utter a word even in justification of her own father ; and she was therefore obliged to listen in silence to much that grieved and wounded her feelings.

" My father was very unfortunate," she observed timidly. "I know he spoke of great misfortunes having encompassed his life."

" Oh yes; but he deserved them all. Neither he nor your mother had any sense; and then their school, which they were obliged to set up—all went to the bad. Paul Stutzer was always weak —he let his pupils do as they pleased, and murder each other, and commit all sorts of wickedness."

" Murder each other, aunt?"

"Yes. Did you never hear about that? One boy actually committed murder while under his care —a horrid boy—I forget his name now; but it was Bennett, or Bond, or something like that. William—no James Bond—that was the name, I am sure ; but at all events he was the ruin of your father, for nobody would trust a boy with him again, for fear he'd let them be murdered, or turn murderers themselves. Oh your father was dreadfully silly !"

"My dear father!" thought Lizette, burying her face in her hands for an instant

"Are you sleepy, child?" demanded her grand-aunt, watching her narrowly; "your eyes look red."

"Yes, aunt, I feel fatigued, and, if you will permit me, I will retire to my room."

"Of course I'll permit you," replied Mrs. Bromley, rising to lead the way from the apartment.

She conducted her to a chamber of moderate size, containing a large, old-fashioned bedstead, hung with blue-checked curtains of a very damp, fusty odour, and covered with a thick coating of dust; a painted toilet table, bearing a cracked looking-glass, of an oval shape, with much of the quicksilver rubbed off here and there in large patches, so that in no part of it could Lizette see the whole of her face at once. At one side her nose would appear as if half cut off, while at the other her forehead and mouth would be invisible.

There was a basin-stand and one or two chairs,
which Miss Stutzer was half afraid to sit on, lest
she might fall through them.   Some cobwebs,
which seemed to be a kind of family insignia,
hung suspended from the ceiling, gracefully sway-
ing to and fro with a gentle movement, as Lizette
walked over the trembling, creaking boards,
which were altogether uncarpeted, with large
chasms in them made by rats.   Well, indeed,
had Mrs. Bromley written, that neither elegance
nor grandeur was to be expected under her roof;
and she might have added that neither were
cleanliness nor neatness to be found there, for
assuredly they were not.   After her experience
of the order and regularity at Meiklam's Rest,
and the elegance of Markham House, the shabbi-
ness and dreariness of Lonehill were very striking
and oppressive to her ; and it can hardly be
wondered at that she wept some bitter tears
before falling asleep that night.

CHAPTER II.

MRS. BROMLEY'S IDEAS ON SOME SUBJECTS.

THE dark November morning that succeeded the night of Lizette's arrival at Lonehill did not much improve the general appearance of things there, when she arose next day. Outwardly and inwardly everything looked very dreary and dirty. The avenue in front of the house was ill gravelled, and the grass borders, of which Mrs. Bromley had proved herself so careful the evening before, did not present any remarkably neat appearance; there were very few trees or shrubs to be seen;

and the garden, which was within a short walk of
the house, only contained some fruit trees, vege-
tables, and weeds.   There were no ornamental
plants or rosebushes to be met with anywhere;
no spot gave promise of flowers for the summer.
Lonehill had formerly been in possession of a
common farmer, that held the place as a tenant
of Mrs. Bromley, who had been the owner of a
large tract of country ; but, when she lost the
greater part of her fortune, and sold estate after
estate to pay off debts, she retained this dismal
spot for her own abode, repairing there as soon as
Farmer Gill's lease had expired.   No one was
ever less humbled or cast down by pecuniary
misfortunes than Mrs. Bromley.   She was just as
proud as ever, though reduced from great wealth
to a very limited income indeed ; and had any
one dared to treat her with less deference than
they had paid her in former days, when she held
sway as lady of the manor, and supreme head of

the peasantry around, her fury would have burst
forth with volcanic force; but no once dared to do
so ; and the peasant women courtesied, and their
husbands touched their hats, with respectful
salutes, whenever Mrs. Bromley appeared out of
doors, just as they had done before her grandeur
was laid low; while she, on her part maintaining
all the dignity of past power, returned their
obeisances and marks of deference with much
condescension, bowing to them in a regal manner
from her old jingling carriage as she drove by.

Lizette was rather surprised to see Martin
Hicks, the man who had driven her from Clicksthorp to Lonehill, and whom Mrs. Bromley
had declared she would turn off instantly, going
about the place very composedly, digging in the
garden, and wheeling a barrow in and out of it
with unconcern, while his mistress gave him
directions as to what he was to do that day and
the next, as if nothing particular had occurred;

and she was equally astonished to see Simon
Peggs making his appearance on the premises,
and receiving a friendly, patronizing shake of
the hand from the lady who had ordered him out
of her house the evening before. However, as
time wore on, she discovered that her grandaunt's
fits of anger were not much regarded by any one
who knew her well; they never failed to terrify
delinquents at the moment of outburst, but they
did not cause lasting offence or mortification.
Simon Peggs was a particular favourite at Lonehill, and Lizette soon learned to regard him as
a truly estimable character. It was his particular delight to talk over his past life, when he
worked as a day labourer, eating his meals, often
of bread and water, out in the fields, under a
burning sun, and toiling from morning till night
like a slave. He loved to compare that time
with his present affluence and comfort; and
brightly, indeed, his small eyes sparkled, as he

told Lizette how his daughters could play the piano as well as any ladies in the land, and how his sons were well-educated young men—one practising as a medical student, the other already a much-respected schoolmaster. "And I believe firmly, Miss Stutzer," he said, "that Providence did it all for me. I never consider for a moment that it was any chance, luck, or fate, or anything of that sort, but God's own doing. I was a poor sickly child; my parents did not love me as well as my brothers and sisters, for I was no ornament to the family, only a blot on it, you may say, for all the rest were fine handsome youngsters. I wasn't given an education like the rest; I wasn't sent to school, or taught anything; I was made the drudge of the house, and I don't say it in anger or vexation, for surely it could not be denied I was an unsightly object, not likely to win the love of mortal, for I had a peevish cross-grained temper

along with the deformity, and I was sulky and
revengeful of injury up to the time of my
twentieth year. Well, I worked as a day
labourer when my father died, away in the fields
of strangers, a poor despised lad, looked down
upon by everybody. And so it came to pass
that a young girl, overworked in one of the
factories at ——, came to our neighbourhood, to
try working in the open air instead of pent up
in those dark prisons, and she was a most beautiful creature, though worn pale and like a shadow.
She came in the haymaking time, and she'd be
tired sooner than any other woman in the fields,
and the overseer would shout constantly to her
to see to herself and be sharper; but I'd see that
she couldn't go faster, and so I'd help her instead
of laughing at her, for I had as much strength
as the biggest lad among them; and so you see,
Miss Stutzer, she took a fancy to me, ugly and
all as I was; and she had great education com-

pared to me, and she taught me to read and write; and after a time we were married; and we prospered from the day of the wedding, when Mr. Hopewell, the clergyman, gave us a present of fifteen guineas, and took us to live in his gate-lodge, with a garden and grass for a cow."

"I must go and see your wife, Mr. Peggs," said Lizette, her eyes sparkling with the tears this simple narration had called forth.

"Ah, Miss, she isn't what she was in our young days," replied Simon, looking sorrowful; "her hair is as white as snow now, and she is a cripple from infirmity brought on by the long factory work. But what does that signify? It is God's doings, and she is satisfied. Her daughters are her treasures now, and every comfort that money can purchase is hers. But you see, Miss Stutzer, there's always a dark spot somewhere, let every thing seem fair and shining —a spot that tells us we can't expect things to last perfect in this life. We must always be put in mind of the journey that's coming to the other world for every one of us. All the money I'm master of couldn't make my Mary walk across the meadow before our house; yet, in their way, riches are a good thing, well used, though they can never turn aside the afflicting hand of the Almighty."

Lizette fully determined that she would make the acquaintance of the Peggs' family; but she soon found that her grandaunt was not disposed to let her visit any one, poor or rich, in the neighbourhood. Occasionally the old lady told her tales of the past, and very proudly her eye would glance around, as she spoke of her old Norman ancestor who had come over with William the Conqueror, a gallant knight, and of how renowned for sense and cleverness all her family had always been—renowned as statesmen and men of learning; and Lizette could not help thinking that if her forefathers had been thus distinguished, they certainly did not derive their distinction for leading such a life as their worthy descendant chose to adopt,—although, like a great many other people in the world, she considered herself entitled to honour and respect, because her ancestors had won the admiration of kings, princes, and people, for virtues and qualities which she certainly never dreamed of imitating herself. She would, no doubt, have thought it a hard case, if, because various of her progenitors had been hung for disgraceful crimes, she was to be looked down upon, after the lapse of generations, with an eye of contempt, shunned by all virtuous individuals, though perfectly innocent of such crimes herself; yet she firmly believed the glory of her revered ancestors should invest her with much distinction, and that, owing to their renown, she was a more respect-able individual than some poor " upstart " who was working his brain away to make himself a name in the present day.

In many ways Lizette's life at Lonehill was dreary in the extreme ; her grandaunt had very few books, and those she had she would rarely allow her to read ; she said women ought to eschew all literary pursuits, as they never could be of any use to them, and, therefore, she kept the key of her old black bookcase carefully hid out of the way. She also had a horror of letter writing, and when her grandniece was seen with a pen in her hand she was generally impatient, and sometimes quite angry. " No man or woman ever came to good that wrote long letters," she frequently said; " it is a proof of a silly brain.   Never write, except just short to the purpose, for if you spin out your sentences, it shows you are either cunning and deceitful, wanting to gloss the truth over with lies, or a fool writing wide of the mark."   This reasoning, however, failed to convince Miss Stutzer in the least.

Mrs. Bromley would not allow her to employ herself in any way to benefit the poor of the neighbourhood; she objected to her visiting the sick for fear of bringing diseases into the house, and she strongly condemned her wish of attending church every Sunday, declaring that once in six weeks was quite often enough to go to public worship, just to set an example to the lower orders ; and she frequently made excuses to keep Lizette at home on Sundays, by saying the horse was lame and wanted a shoe, or that the harness was gone all out of repair in a sudden and inexplicable manner; for the church being no nearer than Clicksthorp, more than four miles off, the young girl could not possibly walk so far. No visitor higher in grade than Simon Peggs ever came to the house. Mrs. Bromley had ceased to hold communion with any gentry in the neighbourhood, as she only liked having people round her who would regard her with supreme deference.

The post office not being nearer than Clicks-thorp, a messenger was only dispatched there for letters once a week.

CHAPTER III.

MORE ABOUT MRS. BROMLEY.

OCCASIONALLY Lizette was gratified by receiving affectionate communications from Miss Pilmer, who, like her cousin, Dillon Crosbie, had the gift of writing well; and she described the different places that she passed through in Italy with great vigour and minuteness, giving clear and amusing accounts of people and things. Very seldom Lizette could answer these letters in peace, for Mrs. Bromley was constantly going about the house, scarcely quiet for a moment, displaying

her remarkable activity of foot from morning till
night; and she was ready at any instant to dart
into any room, while she was continually making
demands upon her niece's services, either in the
matter of darning holes in table-cloths, hemming
kitchen rubbers of strangely coarse fabric, or
patching old chair covers. Indeed, there was
nothing Lizette was not called upon to assist in,
from the setting of a mouse-trap to the shaking
of a dusty carpet.   Notwithstanding all the cats
and kittens maintained at Lonehill, the house
was infested by rats and mice, insomuch that the
former vermin could be heard squealing and
cutting at wainscots, even while people were
talking loudly within their hearing. Lizette often
heard rats trotting playfully round her room as
she lay awake at night, and it was only when she
bethought her of getting one of the gleaming-
eyed black cats to remain in her chamber, that
this nuisance ceased; though the remedy was

nearly as bad as the evil, for she had rather a dread of those sinister sable animals. When she became a little reconciled to the strange mode of life at her grandaunt's house, the past seemed to her like a fairy dream that had been dispelled for ever. Often she felt thankful that Providence had committed her in childhood to the care of Mrs. Meiklam rather than to that of Mrs. Bromley, who certainly seemed very unfitted to take charge of a young person of tender years. She was exceedingly ignorant, most obstinate, and very unreasonable in all her exactions. She could not understand why her niece should like to be so much alone in her room, instead of running about superintending some domestic work, or taking never-ending interest in the farming operations going on out of doors. Never having been accustomed to devote hours of solitude to study or reflection herself, she thought Lizette must either be ill or in the sulks, when she sat thus in retire-

ment. There are many people who cannot comprehend how necessary moments of rest and
quietude are to the minds of others, and very
wearying it is to be in the house with such strong-
nerved individuals. Lizette could not help wondering often how a person, who must have been
accustomed to refinement, and even luxury, at
one time of her life, and not very long ago either,
could so soon lose all ideas of comfort and elegance. Sometimes it seemed to her as if Mrs.
Bromley revelled in doing strange things. She
would wash her face and hands in an old wooden
bowl, rather than in a proper basin, though there
were plenty of basins in the house. She would
not allow the rooms of the house to be swept except upon rare occasions, and once when the
young girl attempted to clean and dust the cobwebs
off the pictures in the parlour, she grew so breathless with rage and excitement, that Lizette feared
she would burst a blood-vessel on the spot, or

fall down in an apoplectic fit.   To say the truth,
however, Mrs. Bromley did not often get into
passions with her niece ; she bore more from her
than she did from any one else, and perhaps it
was for the purpose of paying her marked attention, and displaying her interest in her welfare
and happiness, that she was continually breaking
in upon her solitary musings, and requesting her
to go and "amuse" herself by seeing Poll
Hindman make the butter, or feed the fowl, or
by making observations upon Martin Hicks
putting down cabbage plants in the garden.

The poor girl used to dread the sound of her
grand aunt's stentorian voice shouting to her, as
she often did, all through the house at intervals,
as she was moving on towards her room.
"Lizzy! Lizzy! where are you, Lizzy?"   For
she would not call her by that "horrid, abominable
foreign name, Lizette, that always put her in
mind of a lizard."   Strange to say, although

Mrs. Bromley had lived for many years in France she did not know how to speak a correct sentence in the language of that country; and her opinion of the French people was, that they were all rogues and unprincipled wretches.

"I never liked foreigners," she politely informed Lizette. "Let them be German, or Italian, or French, or any nation except English, and that's bad enough, God knows. If your father hadn't been a foreigner with that outlandish name Stutzer, I never would have quarrelled with him half as often as I did—let him be ever so mean and low; but I couldn't bear the thoughts of his being a German."

"And yet you lived a long time in a foreign country, Aunt?"

"Oh, I was obliged to do it. I couldn't bear to stay in England when I lost my property first; but I grew out of that feeling. I was determined no one should dare to show me they des-

pised me for my poverty.   I would let them know
that nothing could humble me, and so I came
back at last and chose to live at Farmer Gill's
old house here, and I'm not one bit ashamed of
it—not a bit."

" It is always well for us to submit cheerfully
to the will of Providence," remarked Lizette.

" Oh, but it wasn't out of any religious notion
that I grew reconciled to my losses; it was all pride,
the pride that my family always were remarkable
for.   How your mother happened to be so mean I
never could understand, for Paul Stutzer was no
such beauty as to turn any woman's head; he
was a small, insignificant little fellow, scarcely
higher than the mantelpiece there; he wasn't
much above my shoulder ! "

" But I have heard my father had a great
intellect."

" Oh, may be he had, as far as learning goes;
but he hadn't common sense.   Nobody ever has

that reads too much Greek or Latin; it muddles
the brain. I hardly ever knew an Oxford or
Cambridge scholar of note that wasn't half
mad."

CHAPTER IV.

LIZETTE PREPARES TO LEAVE LONEHILL.

DAYS passed; week by week, and month by month old time rolled on till the winter was all gone. The summer only brought green leaves and greener grass to adorn Lonehill. The cabbage and turnips were very flourishing in the garden, and the corn-fields stretched themselves verdantly far in the distance; but there were no flowers anywhere, save the buttercups and daisies and wild primroses that grew of themselves on the hill sides and in the lonely dingles. Lizette loved even the clover blossoms—the sweet purple feathery blossoms in the meadows; and when the hay-making time came, the perfume of the new dried grass was pleasant to her, though at the same time fraught with sadness and melancholy. The woods of Meiklam's Rest came back to her memory then more vividly than ever, and she would pass many regretful hours sitting in lonely spots, far from the house, when the blackbird's whistle thrilled through the air of the still summer evening, and the bees hummed among the wild roses in the hedges. Sometimes her thoughts would wander to a distant island where the tropical sun shone fiercely—sometimes to the days of her early childhood, when she stood by her dying father's side, and very often to the day when she read that letter given her at Markham through mistake by Bessie Pilmer. Bessie wrote often to her; she was now at Markham, making preparations for her marriage, which was to take place when a year had elapsed after the time of her father's death.   After her wedding she was to travel again on the Continent and return in spring to London.   Lizette answered her letters as often as she could; she had little of an interesting nature to communicate, but she endeavoured to write upon serious subjects to her friend. The good seed might take root some time, and she would scatter it unfailingly—though Bessie never wrote upon these topics herself, or even alluded to the state of her feelings upon any point.   Her letters told of facts and worldly matters; there was nothing sentimental in them.

When the autumn approached Lizette felt sad ; she dreaded the coming of the long winter nights, which could not be rendered cheerful in a house where fires were scanty and candlelight was much grudged.   In November she received the cards which announced to her that Bessie Pilmer was now Lady Bend.   All through the winter the newly-married pair remained at Nice, where Mrs. Pilmer joined them, and in spring they returned, as previously arranged, to England. Lizette contrived, after all, to spend the winter pretty comfortably, by making resolutions to look at the best side of things, and resign herself cheerfully to all that might happen. She persuaded her grandaunt by slow degrees to allow her servants to attend church at least every alternate Sunday ; and although the cobwebs were not to be disturbed as yet, nor the old wooden bowl relinquished for a *comme il faut* wash-hand basin, still Lizette found she was making a sure progress of reformation in her grandaunt's house. In April she was somewhat surprised to receive the following letter from Lady Bend :—

" My DEAREST LIZETTE,—Here we are in London still, and I believe we are to remain so till May, when I am to take up my residence at Darktrees.

I shall expect to have you there with me all the summer, so make up your mind to leave Lonehill early in June.   Indeed I am truly longing to see you.   My cousin, Dillon Crosbie, who has got his company, has lately returned to England, owing to his having fallen most unexpectedly into a nice little property in Ireland, left to him by a relative of his father.   You may know how greatly this good news pleases me, and no doubt you will be interested in it also.   My sister Mary and Mrs. Devenish spent some time with us here ; she is truly a beautiful girl.   Dillon admired her greatly and said he did not think there could be a more lovely creature in London this season.   Everyone thinks highly of her, and Mrs. Devenish believes her to be a perfect ' nonsuch.'   She is taller than I am, with dark eyes and jet black hair, and a very elegant figure.   Mr. Devenish has taken a great fancy to Dillon, and he is going to pay her a visit at Wormley Hall, as soon as his affairs in

Ireland are put in train. Will you write, dear,
and say when I may expect you at Darktrees ?

"Always your attached friend,

"BESSIE."

There was a strange agitation in Lizette's heart
as she read the letter, and her face was very pale,
when she laid it down on her old painted toilet
table. Was she glad that she was invited to Lady
Bend's new home? Was she glad that Dillon
Crosbie had fallen into a good fortune ? Was she
glad that Bessie's sister Mary was lovely and
admired by her cousin, who was invited to pay her
godmother a visit at Wormley Hall? She could
hardly explain herself what it was that made her
tremble so nervously, and her heart flutter like
a bird in a cage ; but surely it was not joy that
made her sigh so heavily, and lie down on her bed
for a long while till she grew composed; that
evening she walked so late in the garden, that her

feet were damp and chill when she returned to the house. She caught cold, and this, added to the perturbed state of her mind, made her a little feverish and decidedly ill next day. Her grand-aunt gave her strange mixtures to drink and heaped blankets over her, and shut up the window of her room tightly, telling her to lay quiet without stirring ; but this was a mandate hard to obey, while the patient's head throbbed, and a burning heat oppressed her, combined with great restless-ness. For a long time she was very ill indeed, and Mrs. Bromley nursed her very kindly after a fashion of her own, frequently bending over her, as she was dropping into a soft, balmy slumber, to ask in a hoarse whisper, "Are you asleep, Lizzy?" or startling her up to give her some arrow-root or gruel, when rest was what her weary spirit so much longed for. It was already near the end of May when Lizette first had strength to answer Bessie's letter inviting her to Darktrees,

and she was obliged to tell her friend that, owing
to illness, she could not leave Lonehill in June—
indeed, that she could hardly tell when she might
be able to pay her a visit, upon which Lady Bend
wrote back at once to say how distressed she was,
and that Lizette might fix her own time for going
to Darktrees. " Dear Lizette," she wrote at the
end of her letter, " come to me as soon as ever
you feel strong enough to undertake the journey ;
I will not name any time now, since you are so
weak ; but do not forget me, as I shall feel very
sorry if you are not here before the summer is
over. You can just send me a line to say the day
and hour I may expect you."

Very much indeed did Lizette regret that she
was not able to spend all the lovely summer
months at the mansion at Darktrees ; but her
state of health put the matter beyond all question,
as the illness she had suffered from left a weakness
still very distressing. It was late in September

when she thought she might venture to leave
Lonehill, and she then mentioned to Mrs. Bromley
her wish to pay a visit to Lady Bend.

" Humph, who is she ?" asked the old lady.

" Mrs. Pilmer's daughter; a very dear friend of
mine."

" And do you fancy that she really cares about
a person of your means ?"

" Oh, she is a most generous-hearted person ;
she was always most kind to me."

" But she is a greater lady now than before.
Pilmer is a low name, and Miss Pilmer may be
a different person from Lady Bend—a baronet's
wife."

" I do not believe rank or fortune would
ever alter my friend ; she was always noble-
minded."

" Pooh ! depend upon it she's set up now,
quite above all that; never trust her. I know
the world Lizzy. Once a beggar gets on horse-

back he rides, where I can't say—you know yourself."

" But Miss Pilmer always had a large fortune. She was a wealthy heiress."

" Oh, but she hadn't a title. I know the Pilmers must have been merchants originally; and now, when this girl is ' your Ladyship,' take my word for it that she'll make you blush for your inferior station. Don't go to her at all, child ; stay at home here, where you are so happy, with no person to thwart or prevent you doing whatever you please ; no person always reminding you of how low and poor you are."

" Ah, I wish to go, dear Aunt," said Lizette earnestly. " Do no prevent me ; it will grieve me much not to visit my dear friend."

" Mind you come back, then, the moment she affronts you," said Mrs. Bromley, her eye flashing ; " the first insult you are aware of, leave her house."

"Dear Aunt, Bessie will never act as you anticipate," said Lizette smiling; "and now I will write to her and say I am going to her at once."

Mrs. Bromley proposed that her servant man, Martin Hicks, should escort her for part of the journey, to look after her luggage and herself; and Lizette, not having heard from Bessie for some weeks, now despatched a letter to her saying she would leave Lonehill on a certain day, arriving at Bretton Wold, a railway station within ten miles of Sir James Bend's residence, at about three o'clock in the afternoon, from which she would proceed in some other public conveyance to the village of Darktrees. Miss Stutzer was busy completing her preparations for the journey when Lady Bend's answer to her letter arrived, just the day before she was to start. To Lizette it seemed decidedly a constrained one, without spirit or fervour. Perhaps it was only her imagination,

influenced by Mrs. Bromley's late remarks that
made her believe this; but she could not forbear
thinking the letter cold. It is true Bessie
expressed herself politely on the subject of her
friend's visit, yet what if she might not be
welcome at Darktrees after all! Lady Bend wrote
that she would send her own carriage for her to
the railway station at Bretton Wold, to prevent
her being obliged to travel in any public conveyance after leaving the train. This was all very
well, and very attentive, *but Lizette did not show
the letter to her grandaunt.* The postcript of the
letter may have had a depressing influence upon
the young girl. It was as follows : " My sister
is now with me, and also my cousin Dillon
Crosbie; he escorted her from Wormley Hall; as
I am sorry to say Mrs. Devenish died of paralysis
about six weeks ago. She left my sister a large
fortune; so that this, together with what she had
before, renders her very wealthy indeed."

For some time Lizette was inclined to withdraw her promise of visiting Darktrees altogether. She dreaded the thoughts of going there; but what would her grandaunt say if she suddenly altered her mind thus; and, above all, what would Lady Bend think of her, for there was now no time to write back to her and prevent her sending the carriage for her all the way to Bretton Wold. The next day was fixed for the journey, and she thought it better to go than not; so she locked her trunk with trembling fingers, determining to start from Clicksthorp by railway, the following morning.

CHAPTER V.

DARKTREES HALL.

SHE passed a restless night, scarcely sleeping at all, and arose early next day. Mrs. Bromley could not prevail upon her to eat more than a few morsels of breakfast, and the old lady was obliged to console herself by filling a large paper bag with sundry home-made cakes, which she insisted upon her carrying for food on the journey.

It was a bright September day, and the sun shone cheerily, but the young traveller did not

feel light of heart.   She drove to Clicksthorp
in her grandaunt's carriage, accompanied by
Martin Hicks, and was soon safely in the railway carriage.   The journey was not marked
by any peculiar event.   Martin Hicks saved
her the trouble of looking after her luggage,
and indeed made himself very useful as an attendant during the changes from one train to another
that occurred on the way; and thus things went
smoothly enough all the way to Bretton Wold.
Very nervously Lizette's heart beat as the train
neared this station at three o'clock in the afternoon.   She wondered who would come to meet
her there in Lady Bend's carriage.   Would Sir
James himself come, or would somebody else
come?   Puffing, gasping, shrieking, the engine
pushed on to the quiet country station, giving
out great pantings, as it slackened its speed, and
finally stopped.   Here was Bretton Wold.   The
railway porters ran to-and-fro, opening carriages,

D 2

and calling out the name of the place in an un-
intelligibly curtailed manner, while Martin Hicks
appeared for the last time to hand his young lady
out. With a quivering heart she stood on the
platform. A handsome chaise and pair was in
waiting at the station, and an equally handsome
footman approached the young lady, saluting her
respectfully, and asking if she were the lady going
to Darktrees. A footman! No one else was
there to meet her, save the fat coachman on
the carriage box. Pale and weary Lizette replied that she was the lady bound for Lady
Bend's house, and she saw the tall footman looking curiously at Martin Hicks, who was bringing
her trunk himself to the carriage. She got into
the chaise, and having given Martin a donation
and a message for her grandaunt, soon found
herself driving at a quick pace towards the re-
doubtable Darktrees. No one had come to meet
her but the servants. That was the thought that

floated uppermost on her mind as the carriage sped on. Had any gentleman now staying at Darktrees been much interested in her, would he not have taken the trouble of coming to escort her from Bretton Wold? She was glad enough Sir James had not come; but was there not somebody else under Bessie's roof, who might have driven to meet her, if he had cared at all about her? Notwithstanding the sinking state of her spirits, Lizette endeavoured to grow calm as the carriage went on, and by the time the village of Darktrees was reached, the palpitation of her heart had altogether ceased. It was not a pretty village; the houses were generally old, and by no means neat-looking. Clattering and thundering with a noise that made many a window tremble, the handsome chaise dashed through its one long street, while cottagers stared and gaped after it, till passing from their view, it came to

the high dark walls of the demesne of the pro-
prietor.

The country residence of Sir James Bend had,
indeed, been well named, for it was a dark,
castellated house, shadowed by enormous trees,
which grew so near as to cast their gloom upon
the rooms within. A moat had once been round
the building, but late alterations had done away
with the inconvenience and security of this, so
that it was no longer necessary to lift or lower a
drawbridge on the arrival of visitors. As the
carriage drove up the long, dark avenue, Lizette
heard the ceaseless cawing of large birds, mingled
with the rustling of leaves, as the giant trees
swayed backwards and forwards in the evening air,
looking as if they were rocking themselves gently
to-and-fro, while they mused in sadness upon
happier days, when they were first planted, lithe
young saplings there. The steps leading to the

house were of dusky hue, and dotted here and there with spots of moss. Things did not in general look very neatly kept around this gloomy pile. When the carriage stopped a servant appeared at the entrance door, and coming out, stood on the steps, looking on, while the foot-man assisted Miss Stutzer to alight; she entered the wide hall which was hung around with dusty memorials of martial heroes that had long been mingling in dust themselves; and here she was met by a very pompous finely-dressed woman, whose stiff silk gown rustled at every movement. She accosted the young lady with great courtesy, and said: " Lady Bend suffers from headache this evening, but she desired me to conduct you to her dressing-room where she is at present Shall I attend you there?"

" If you please," said Lizette, and she followed this woman in somewhat low spirits, so that the whole of the wide house through which she passed

seemed to her very dismal indeed, though bearing evidence of much antique splendour. The
staircases were wide and of dark, polished oak;
the corridors long and lofty, and the whole route
from the hall to Lady Bend's dressing-room so
intricate that Miss Stutzer was bewildered with
turnings and ante-rooms. At length the goal
was reached; she and her conductress stopped at
a door, and the latter gave a little knock, answered
by a low "come in," faintly uttered by the lady
within. Lizette entered the room, and Lady
Bend met her at the door. In the twilight she
thought her face looked thin and worn, without a
shade of colour on lip or cheek, the hand that
clasped hers was very cold, and likewise the lips
that pressed her own were chill in the extreme,
although the evening was warm, and a fire burning in the dressing-room.

CHAPTER VI.

LADY BEND.

LADY BEND asked her visitor how she was, and how she had travelled, and spoke very kindly indeed; but Lizette could not help observing that her manner was perfectly changed since she had last seen her. The effort to speak to her seemed a labour; sometimes she remained for several minutes without opening her lips, sitting in her chair, and looking into the fire; Lizette asked for Sir James Bend, and learned that he was in Scotland; she asked for her sister and was told

she had gone out to drive with Dillon Crosbie;
and in making this reply a sudden flush overspread Lady Bend's features, lasting for a little
time, and then fading away. Lizette saw it even
in the darkening twilight. Never before had she
felt more ill at ease and *de trop*. How ardently
she wished she had not come there at all! Whenever Lady Bend spoke her voice was gentle and
kind, but Lizette understood enough of her dis-
position to be aware that even though she might
wish to be rid of an unwelcome person's company
she would not speak to anyone rudely or
sharply. She looked very elegant and refined,
in a rich, though negligent morning cos-
tume, which she had not yet changed for a
dinner dress, but all brilliancy of eye was
completely gone, the expression of her whole face
changed. After some time of constrained speaking upon both sides, Lizette went to her room to
change her travelling garments, and attire herself

for the evening, and at about half-past six o'clock she went down to the drawing-room, entering it with great calmness. The blaze of a large fire was the only light that revealed the occupants of the lofty room; but she saw at a glance that Dillon Crosbie and Mary Pilmer were sitting together on a sofa, while Lady Bend sat in an armchair apart from them. As she entered, Captain Crosbie arose and came a little way forward to meet her; but there was little alacrity in his air; indeed it appeared as though he would rather not accost her if he could help it. He shook hands, and hoped, in a tone of marked indifference, that she was well and not fatigued; and then, after placing a chair for her near Lady Bend, took his place once again on the sofa from which he had risen. Mary Pilmer had also stood up on Lizette's entrance, merely giving her a rather haughty inclination of the head, without deigning to bend her majestic person any farther.

In the fire-light she appeared very tall, dark, and
queenly, dressed in some rich fabric, her gown
being made high to the throat; a row of pearls
was fastened behind in her jet-black hair, and
some very dazzling precious stones glittered in
the bracelets round her wrists. After thus coldly
saluting Miss Stutzer, who had never seen her
since she was a proud, overbearing child, she sat
beside Captain Crosbie, and addressed him in a
low tone. Now and then Lady Bend addressed
Lizette, endeavouring evidently to appear as
pleased and attentive as possible, yet failing to
deceive the quick perception of her sensitive
friend. The conversation on the sofa was carried
on in low, grave tones, exclusively by the two
people that occupied it; and Lady Bend seemed
careful of not allowing Miss Stutzer to take much
note of her sister and Dillon Crosbie. When
dinner was announced, Captain Crosbie arose and
stood hesitatingly for a moment in the middle of

the room, as if undecided as to whom he should
conduct from the drawing-room.   Lizette knew
that he looked towards her, but she heard Lady
Bend saying in a low tone, " You can take my
sister, I shall reserve Miss Stutzer for myself;"
and she drew Lizette's hand within her own arm,
while he with alacrity turned to Mary Pilmer,
and led her first from the room.   At the dinner
table Lizette sat opposite to Captain Crosbie and
Lady Bend's sister, and now in the full glare of
wax-lights, she looked to see what the latter
really was like.   Her eyes were then thrown down,
displaying the long silken lashes that fringed
them; her features were certainly beautifully
formed, her nose faultless, and the mouth well
cut, though rather haughty in expression. Lizette
thought her decidedly very handsome and was
still watching her with admiration, when she
raised her eyes and fixed them full upon her
face.   Lizette could hardly explain the nature of

the feeling that struck her as Mary's gaze met hers, but it certainly was not a pleasant one ; she lowered her own eyes quickly by instinct, but felt impelled to raise them soon again, and look once more at Miss Pilmer's face ; but the expression of it had now changed, and Mary was calmly looking on the table-cloth. When Lizette turned her eyes from the contemplation of Mary's countenance, by a sort of entanglement they caught a very fixed, scrutinizing look from Captain Crosbie, which caused her to lower them a little, thus preventing her from seeing that he instantly turned his gaze from her to Mary. Lady Bend seemed wofully ill at ease, flushing often for no apparent cause, and sometimes becoming quite pale again. Now and then she roused herself to speak cheerfully to Lizette, who had no spirits or animation to enliven the conversation herself, or prevent it flagging as it often did. When Dillon spoke, he generally addressed either of his cousins; and to Miss Stutzer it seemed very apparent that he purposely and palpably avoided all conversation with herself. Had he grown proud now, because he was a rich man; and did he despise her because she was a dependent on a poor old grandaunt? She was afraid that such might be the case, and the idea was a mortifying one.

After dinner everyone returned to the drawing-room, for Captain Crosbie did not remain behind to linger over the wine, perhaps because he had no gentleman to keep him company; and now, as before, all his attention was directed to Mary Pilmer, who immediately began to search among her music-books, and then having found a favourite piece, went to the piano at once, without consulting the wish of any one present, and not paying the least attention to the visitor so lately arrived. Dillon arranged the music-seat

for her and opened the piano with all due politeness, and when she was seated at the instrument,
he never left her side, turning the music sheets
for her, and uttering commendatory observations
on the skilfulness of her playing, till she was
tired of performing, and abandoned her seat at the
piano. Her execution was very masterly, but
Lizette would have preferred more softness and
sweetness of touch. No one asked herself to
play or sing, nor did Lady Bend approach the
piano that evening. It was decidedly very dull
—the conversation unconnected and flat—nobody
laughed, or even smiled; there was no reading—
no needle-work. If this was the result of grandeur, Lizette felt it was decidedly a melancholy
one. She had a firm conviction that if she had
been the poorest dependant, or even a menial
brought unexpectedly into the company of her
superiors, she could not have been treated with

more coldness and constraint than she now was. "Why did I come at all?" was the burden of her thoughts, ringing through her brain throughout the evening like the chimes of a doleful bell.

When coffee was over she was relieved when Lady Bend asked if she would not like to retire early to rest, though at the same time she could not help thinking that the question sounded very like a hint that her hostess would like to get rid of her with all imaginable speed. "Yes, I should like very much to retire," she replied; "I am much fatigued.

"Dillon, will you be good enough to ring for candles?" said Lady Bend. But Dillon did not hear; he was too much engaged by something Mary was saying to him. Bessie arose herself and touched the bell, and as she did so, a smothered sigh escaped her. Mary now addressed her sister in a gay tone, and laughed at something

that was amusing her. Bessie joined her immediately, and they both laughed together ; but Lizette could not hear what either said. In the
meantime a servant answered the bell. Bessie
ordered a maid to be summoned with candles ;
she was still laughing and smiling with her sister,
and looking at her with much of tenderness and
affection beaming in her eyes. Lizette sat far off in
silence; for though Captain Crosbie was not now
talking to Mary, he stood near the fireplace looking on the ground, just as if Miss Stutzer were
not present, or at all events unworthy of any
notice. She felt awkward in the extreme. Indeed
it surprised her that Lady Bend could betray so
much ill-breeding as to laugh and talk with her
sister in low tones which were inaudible to
other ears. When a maid-servant appeared with
lights, Lady Bend did not move from beside her
sister, but merely said—

" Pray show Miss Stutzer to her room ; I hope there is a fire in it."

Lizette arose, finding it hard to check the tears fast rising to her eyes, and hastily approached to say " good night" to her hostess.   Bessie kissed her fervently, and pressed her hand in silence, but Mary scarcely acknowledged her more than by a little haughty bow, which told of more contempt than no notice whatever could have expressed.   Lizette merely vouchsafed a bow and a faint " good night" to Captain Crosbie, who never moved from his position near the mantelpiece, and then left the room with the attending maid.   This young woman happened to be very chatty and good-natured, but Lizette remarked that she went through the corridors and up the great stair-cases at a hurried pace, once or twice starting visibly when any noise struck upon her ear, and when the clock rang out the hour of ten,

just as they were near the end of their journey
she nearly let the candlestick fall out of her hand
with an involuntary exclamation, " Oh, Lord, but
that scared me !''

CHAPTER VII.

WEIRD SIGHTS AND SOUNDS.

THEY stopped at a large chamber, furnished hand-somely with heavy antique tables, chairs, and bedstead.   There was tapestry in abundance, and figured velvet hangings, and much other adorn-ments of a rich and sombre kind.

" This is a wild, large house ma'am, ain't it ? " asked the chatty maiden, shivering evidently, though it was not cold, as they were within this apartment.

" Yes, it seems a fine old building."

" Dear me, it's as ancient as I don't kuow what. I'm sure it's a wonder to me why people think old houses fine; if I was the queen I'd have them all pulled dowu, ma'am, every one that was above a hundred years old.   As for this house, ma'am, I believe it's nigh as old as Noah's ark, and all the dreadful stories there's about it! Oh dear, I'm sorry I ever hired in it at all! "

" There are always foolish stories about old houses."

" Yes, ma'am, about ghosts, and spirits, and such like."

" And I suppose it is reported that there are ghosts here?" said Lizette, who felt that if ever ghosts haunted any earthly spot, this was the very place for them.

" Indeed, ma'am, they say it's surely haunted."

" But you don't believe that, of course ? "

" Believe it, ma'am ! I wish I didn't.   I think my quarter will never be up till I get away entirely out of it.   I'm trembling every night of my life like an aspen; and there isn't one about the place that don't believe it's haunted, except maybe the mistress herself, poor thing ! "

" But surely no one about the place ever saw anything supernatural ? "

" Well, ma'am, people don't like to mention such things, but since you ask a straight question I won't deny that I did."

" It must have been fancy—you may be sure of that."

" It was no fancy, ma'am ; for John Lacy, the under-butler, saw it too, when I called him up, to look at it, and he turned as white as paper too, though he isn't a man to say easy frightened. We both watched it together, and it glided before our very eyes—oh, awful, ma'am ! till it was hid from our sight."

" And what was it like ? " asked Lizette, who felt a little amused.

"Oh, all white, ma'am; a regular ghost, and its feet quite bare. I creep all over when I think of it."

"When did you fancy you saw it?"

"Ah, ma'am, don't say 'fancy,' it's a sin, for John Lacy and me both saw it as plain as I see you this minute, and for a long while too. It was just about a fortnight ago. You know, ma'am," added the girl lowering her voice and speaking gravely, as she stirred up the fire in the ample grate—"you know, ma'am, it's said about here that no marriage of any of the gentlemen that this place belonged to has turned out well or happy, since ages ago that one of the old baronet's wives was poisoned by a wretched woman among her own servants—her lady's-maid, I believe; and so they say the ghost of the murdered lady goes about the place after any new bride of the owner comes first to live at Darktrees. It's awful to think of it, ma'am;

and there's another dreadful story along with that one. Do you know Sir James Bend well, ma'am?"

"No, not very well."

"It's of the mistress you are the friend, I believe?"

"Yes; Lady Bend and I were long friends."

" "Poor young lady—she's so lovely too; but maybe she doesn't know that her husband's what he is. It's a fact, ma'am, that he was tried for murder once in his life!"

"Murder!" repeated Lizette in surprise.

"Ah, ma'am; he was tried, but he wasn't hung; he killed a young gentleman at school away in a county near this—hit him a blow in a passion and he never spoke again, and that was the ruin of his master I hear, for nobody liked the school after it; and sure, ma'am, some says the ghost of the poor murdered boy is seen on moonlight nights going moaning round and

round the grounds here. I can't say I ever saw
that, but the lady's ghost I saw and no doubt at
all, though I wouldn't for the world let her ladyship know it."

All at once the mystery that had long puzzled
Lizette was solved. The name of Bend familiar
to her infant ears was the name of that unfortunate boy who her grandaunt told her had
been the cause of her father's ruin as a schoolmaster. Strange chance that had linked her dear
friend's fate with that of this individual! Yet
not stranger than many other chances of this
mortal life. Who is there that can say they
have not known of real occurrences within their
own experience which they would not have believed possible if narrated by the pen of the
novelist?

Lizette thought the chatty maid, Martha
Skelton, had now talked enough; but she saw
the girl was anxious to linger as long as possible

in the room, pretending to arrange different things and helping her to put on her dressing gown; while she was in reality only wishing to delay the dismal necessity of traversing those wide, dark corridors, on her way to the servants' hall. But at length she took her departure, leaving the young lady sitting *en deshabille* in a very comfortable chair before the fire, a very large blazing one, cheering to behold. When she was gone Lizette became plunged in a sad reverie that lasted long; she sat leaning back in the old chair, dreamily looking into the fire, forgetting that hour after hour must be passing; for her ears were not yet sufficiently accustomed to the general sounds of the house to admit of her noting the ponderous clock in a distant corridor tolling out the hours in a mournful, slow manner, that sounded more like the measured ring of a funeral bell than the ordinary striking of a clock; neither did she think of looking at the little timepiece hanging over her mantel-piece, whose hands were going round and round steadily and ceaselessly, till they had measured many a sixty minutes in succession, from the time she had first sat there buried in profound thought. The fire, large as it had been, dropped off into embers, and the warm blaze had all died out; the waxlights on the toilet table were burning still, though considerably diminished in length. At last it struck her that she had better rouse herself and get into bed, and just as she was moving from her chair, a noise outside the window attracted her. She listened attentively; there were decidedly some sounds like little taps against the glass, and these seemed to be followed by a voice distinctly whispering in low, weird accents, "Do you know what murder is? Do you know what death is?" On looking at the time-piece she saw that it was now long past midnight, almost on the stroke of one. Without the slightest feeling of superstition in

her heart, our young friend could not help feeling afraid. Might not such things as ghosts
exist? Who could affirm positively that they
did not? But no; she must put such ridiculous
folly out of her head. She must have been mistaken; the sounds were probably caused by the
wind rustling among the trees outside. Hush!
There were repeated little raps at the window
pane, and again those mysterious, unearthly
sounding tones, low but distinct, " Do you know
what murder is—do you know what death is?"
Her frame grew cold as ice—drops of chill perspiration gathered on her forehead. For a
minute she felt as if palsied. But she must
shake off this coward fear. She boldly walked
to the window, and drawing aside the heavy
curtains looked upon the scene without. The
moon was shining brightly on the raised balcony
outside the window which could be reached by
steps from the ground beneath. Near and far she

beheld ivy-covered trees, low brushwood, tangled copses and long grass growing rank and uncropped mingled with very tall, sturdy weeds. All without was clearly defined, as if it were noonday. Unable to see anything likely to account for the mysterious whispers she had heard, she was about to turn from the window when she beheld something white fluttering, as it were, among the branches of trees far off. It might have been the delusion of fancy; but it certainly seemed to her as if a white figure were making rapid movements, winding itself in and out through trees at a distance—so far off that she could not distinctly distinguish what the apparition was like; but that it was really there, she did not doubt, though she speedily brought herself to the conclusion that it could be possibly accounted for in some very commonplace way; perhaps it was only a sheet hanging out to dry, and fluttering in the night air, though if

Lizette had bethought of it, she would have known that there was no wind stirring abroad, hardly a breeze at present to shake the moonlit trees. Setting aside all superstitious feelings, and assuring herself that sitting up late and the journey of the day, together with her sad reflections, had bewildered both ears and eyes, she closed her shutters, drew the massive curtains once more across the window, and undressed for bed. The waxlights were extinguished, and she endeavoured to sleep, though for a long while strange fancies floated through her brain, keeping her in a wakeful, excited state. But she slept at last long and heavily.

CHAPTER VIII.

GREAT UNHAPPINESS.

NEXT day the bright sun dispelled many of the
gloomy fancies and visions that had been haunting Miss Stutzer's mind the previous night ; but
still she felt far from happy or at ease, and she
almost dreaded appearing in the breakfast-room ;
she dressed herself nervously, being assisted by
Martha Skelton, the chatty ghost-seeing friend of
the previous night; but she took care not to mention having heard or observed anything remarkable
during the hours that had intervened since they

separated. To the hope expressed that she had slept well she answered, " very well indeed," and Martha only gave a long-drawn sigh, inwardly breathing a prayer, not heard by the young lady she was assisting to dress. In the breakfast parlour, which, like other rooms at Darktrees, was very large and curiously fashioned, she met Lady Bend, who was sitting in one of the large bow-windows of the apartment, looking rather abstracted as her guest suddenly broke in upon her reverie. She blushed, started, and then turned pale, as she extended her hand with a forced smile saying,

" Good morning, Lizette ; I hope you were comfortable last night."

" Oh, yes," replied Miss Stutzer, who did not like to speak of what she deemed her foolish fancies ; " I passed a very good night as far as sleep was concerned."

" I am glad to hear it ; I am afraid you will

think Darktrees very dull.   In summer it looks
better than now since autumn is coming on."

"It seems a very fine old place," replied
Lizette; "you used to like ancient feudal man-
sions long ago. Does not this one just suit
you?"

"It is ancient enough certainly," observed
Bessie evasively, and then, ceasing to speak, her
gaze seemed fixed upon the window ; Lizette's
glance followed hers, and she observed Captain   Crosbie   with   Mary   Pilmer   leaning
on   his   arm   passing   the   window.   They
were both smiling and talking, and Mary appeared
in high spirits. An expression of much pain shot
across Lady Bend's face, but it had passed away
before she turned to speak to Lizette again.

"You must feel very happy to have your sister
with you," said Miss Stutzer, who found it
difficult to find a subject of conversation.

All at once Lady Bend coloured as red as scarlet ; she did not reply for a few seconds ; at last she said,

" You recollect, then, how much I always loved my sister; though we seldom saw each other; it is a mysterious and wonderful bond, this tie of kindred, experienced even in earliest childhood."

A half smothered sigh escaped from the speaker as she concluded her sentence. Very radiant and animated Mary now entered the breakfast room, accompanied by Captain Crosbie, and although she hardly noticed Miss Stutzer at all, she spoke to her sister of the pleasant early walk she had taken, and of how charming the morning was. Again Lizette felt herself decidedly *de trop*, and reduced to a deplorable state of constraint, feeling in the way of every one round her. Dillon Crosbie evidently wishing to avoid her, and her hostess betraying, in spite of great efforts to conceal it, that she was not welcome there. They all sat down to breakfast. " Will you drive to-day,

Dillon?" asked Mary as she was breaking a piece of toast.

" Yes, if you like."

" And you, Bessie ? I wish to show you that exquisite place we visited yesterday. I should quite like a little pic nic there—it is such a lovely spot."

" I am afraid I cannot go, dear Mary," replied Lady Bend gently, and a little mournfully.

" Why not? I am very anxious that you should ; it would do you good."

" You had better come," urged Dillon.

" We can take out the phaeton," resumed Mary ; " it will just hold you and me, and Dillon can drive us. I cannot bear any carriage so well as that nice light phaeton."

A faint glow overspread Lady Bend's face as she replied,

" Perhaps I may go ; I am sure a drive would do me good."

Poor Lizette felt ready to sink under the table with shame and mortification as her hostess spoke. Captain Crosbie was looking down at the table cloth, picking up some crumbs as if absently. Miss Stuzer's eyes were lowered also, so that she did not see the earnest, uneasy gaze that he eventually fixed upon her face. Nobody had asked her to be of the driving party ; indeed how could there be room for her in the phaeton fixed upon by Miss Pilmer? Lizette thought she must make up her mind to be treated, palpably, undis guisedly as a person of inferior rank ; and it was a bitter conviction, even to her most humble of hearts. Once or twice the thought struck her that some one might have been maligning her to Lady Bend. Was not Luke Bagly her enemy? What might he not have said of her to his mis- tress ; he so cunning and hypocritical, and believed by Bessie to be truthful and honest? Why had she not openly told her friend her opinion of that dangerous man, who might now be slandering herself? Yet could Lady Bend have altered so much within a year as to turn against her thus? No, she could not believe it; Bessie was not a person who would credit malicious reports without seeking for their foundation. Alas! she feared it was pride and prosperity that had worked all this sad change in her former friends. Had not her aunt warned her of it? Ah, why had she rejected the wise old lady's advice? When the letter bag was brought in, Mary opened it first, and commenced reading the newspaper, which had just arrived. Lady Bend seemed nervously anxious for letters, and her colour came and went fitfully, as she watched Dillon looking at the directions of a great many letters, which Mary had given to him from the post-bag. None, however, were for her; they were all for Captain Crosbie himself—a goodly supply too. Soon Mary flung down the newspaper, and said she would like to drive early, upon which her sister said they might go at once and dress, and they left the room together, Mary taking her sister's arm as they did so.

And now Lizette was alone with Captain Crosbie. Frightful moment! But woman's dignity upheld her in the trying situation; she could not help feeling hurt by his indifference, and surely the treatment of everyone in the house had given her cause for being mortified. As soon as the ladies had left the room he approached her, and made a remark upon a strange-looking old tree just outside the window, near which she had withdrawn when breakfast was over. She answered coldly, and although he now manifested an evident desire to make amends for past inattention by speaking with animation and endeavouring to keep up a spirited conversation, she repelled his efforts. If he was ashamed to talk openly to her in presence of the proud Mary Pilmer, she certainly would not encourage him to do so in secret. No, she was not mean enough for that. All his observations fell flat to the ground ; and at length Lizette quitted the room altogether. She went up stairs, and was contemplating some old pictures on one of the intricate corridors above when, by an unfortunate *contretemps,* she heard Lady Bend's voice speaking somewhere near, though she herself was unseen. The words Lizette heard were very distinct, and evidently addressed to Captain Crosbie, who must have left the breakfast-room just after herself. Lady Bend's soft voice, which the peculiar construction of the corridor must have borne to her unseen listener's ears, with more clearness than the tones would have permitted in any other place, gave utterance to this sentence—-

" If Lizette Stutzer were out of the house all might be well enough ; every hour, Dillon, I wish she had not come ; but you know I cannot tell her so. Mary, too, says she thinks it is an insult to her my having her here; what can I do?"

What Dillon answered Lizette waited not to hear; but faint and sad she gained her own room as quickly as possible. Now were not all her former miserable suspicions confirmed? Oh, wretched misfortune and obstinacy that had brought her to Darktrees at all! Oh, mortifying words that she had heard thus spoken of her by her once kind friend Bessie! In the first moments of her anguish she thought she would leave the house on the spot, and travel back to Lonehill; she thought she would give back the twenty pounds Lady Bend had given to her at their last parting in London. She thought she would go to her at once, and say that she was willing to rid her of the intrusion that she unfortunately and unconsciously had forced upon her. The poor girl was fearfully excited; but her emotion after a time subsided. She determined that she would remain for one whole week at Darktrees, when she would take her departure calmly, without exciting in Lady Bend's mind any suspicion of her having overheard her mortifying words to Dillon Crosbie. She was walking up and down her room when Lady Bend with her bonnet on, entered, looking flushed and hurried.

" My dear Lizette," she said in an agitated voice, " will you excuse my leaving you for a little while. I have been ill lately, and obliged to drive out every day. The gardens are open and there are some fine greenhouse plants which you——"

" Are you ready, Bessie ?" called out the impatient voice of Captain Crosbie, sounding loudly through the echoing corridors.

" Good bye, Lizette," and pressing her burning, parched lips to her visitor's cheek, Bessie ran away so quickly that she did not even close the door after her. She was evidently much confused. When she was gone Lizette felt mollified; it was showing her *some* mark of respect, at least, to apologise; it was not quite so bad as if Lady Bend had gone off without saying anything to excuse herself. But oh, those dreadful words on the corridor! How ardently she wished that she could fancy some of Martha Skelton's phantoms had breathed them in her ear. Hearing the grating of wheels on the avenue beneath the window, she looked out, and saw a beautiful new phaeton drawn by elegant-looking ponies, sparkling and flashing in the sunlight, as it lightly drove by, containing Lady Bend and her sister, who were both dressed expensively—the latter especially so; with rich parasols deeply fringed, shading such bonnets, as people of moderate fortune only see in milliners' warerooms, or on heads of the very wealthy,

with whom they do not consort.   Captain Crosbie
was driving them, and a servant was in attendance, holding a basket which contained good
things for luncheon.

CHAPTER IX.

THE LIBRARY AT DARKTREES.

LEFT to herself, Lizette could not compose her mind sufficiently to work or read ; she passed an hour or two of very painful meditation; and at the end of that time was summoned to luncheon by the very fine house-keeper, Mrs. Polworth, who was most attentive and respectful, expressing her supposition that Miss Stutzer was too much fatigued after her late journey to accompany the ladies on their drive, observing that Lady Bend had been ordered a great deal of exercise in the open air, which was, no doubt, meant as a sort of apology for the young visitor being thus left alone while her hostess went off upon a pleasure excursion. Mrs. Polworth, after luncheon, offered to show Miss Stutzer the library, if she were fond of reading, and Lizette was very willing to accompany her to it. The woman then left her, closing her in, upon a great collection of books indeed, arranged with very little regard to order. Several strewed the tables, and a few were resting on the floor; there was a great deal of dust everywhere, and the windows had a black, dim look; there were queer statues in the corners of the room, undraped and fantastic, and many pictures on the walls which had better not have been there, or anywhere else, either. Lizette sat down and took up a volume from the table; she opened it, perceiving at once that it was a French work of an infidel character, openly maintaining that there is no future, no resurrection, no afterlife. With a shudder she turned to see the name of the author of the work, and in doing so, her eye lit upon these words written at the head of the title page in a bold, firm hand: "Dillon Crosbie, from his most ardently attached friend and betrothed, Mary Pilmer."

The volume dropped from her hand, and for many moments she sat confounded in a wretched stupor, unable to think collectedly of anything. Wave upon wave of misery seemed overwhelming her, threatening to engulf her. Had Dillon Crosbie really become a sceptic, and was he about to marry a woman who could offer him such a present as an infidel work of the most subtle and pernicious description? If not altogether an unbeliever himself, was he not perhaps on the brink of uniting his fate with one who must surely entertain infidel opinions? Most deeply grieved she felt; she feared the temptation of riches and the wish of rendering himself still

richer by marrying a girl who possessed immense
wealth, had been too much for Captain Crosbie's
fortitude.   Sad it was to her to reflect upon what
he had been as a boy, apparently noble-hearted,
generous, and most truthful—thinking of others,
and rarely of himself.   It had always appeared
to her that both Bessie and Dillon were gifted
with natures beautifully adapted for receiving the
seed of religious truth, and bringing forth fruit
richly from it, if it could only be planted judi-
ciously in their hearts.   There can be little doubt
that there are some dispositions which even in
their natural state appear more fitted to nourish
and treasure Christian feelings than others.   God
seems sometimes to have been long in preparing
the soil for the reception of the true seed.   How
often have we known and heard of individuals
who for years before they were fully alive to the
direct influence of the truth, still seemed to
harbour every Christian sentiment in their hearts,

while they were in a state of great darkness;
and who subsequently have been kindled into
divine fervour, when the light of the Gospel
torch touched their spirits! There are some
indeed whom God has seemed to have chosen for
his own especial servants from the hour of their
birth, though permitted, for wise purposes, to
remain without knowledge of the truth, till an
appointed time of fitness drew near. It may
be that those who at one period of their lives
have experienced the influence of doubts and
misgivings in their own souls will be better fitted
to comprehend the hearts of unregenerate natures
after they themselves have been kindled into
grace, than many who have been nurtured in
piety from their cradles; they may know where
the great errors lie in the minds of those they
wish to lead to the truth. How long Lizette sat
there in the dim old library, buried in sad, most
bitter thought, she could scarcely have told; but

the bright part of the early day had vanished, and twilight was succeeding to the broader glare of noon before she thought of leaving the room. Suddenly steps were heard approaching, and to her dismay the chief object of her meditations entered. He seemed to feel quite as awkward as herself, and was evidently undecided as to whether he should really come in or retreat again ; but gathering courage he closed the door, the handle of which he had held in his hand for some seconds, and approached Lizette with an air of forced composure.

"We have just come in," he said, speaking cheerfully; "the drive was very pleasant, but Lady Bend was sorry you could not accompany us."

"She is very kind," replied Lizette coldly, and with a tinge of bitterness in her tone which she afterwards regretted.

"Miss Pilmer was very anxious that her sister

should drive out to-day," continued Captain Crosbie after a pause, " only for that I am sure she would not have gone, and then the phaeton only holds two ladies with comfort."

What lame excuses and apologies ! They could not deceive Lizette.

" I had not the least wish to drive out," she returned.

" But you must have been extremely lonely all day by yourself. Really it would have been unpardonable in us, our all deserting you, only that we were obliged to do it."

" I was not very lonely ; I generally find companions in my own thoughts, and they pass many hours of solitude expeditiously enough."

A little pause now ensued during which Captain Crosbie stooped to pick up the French book which Miss Stutzer had forgotten to lift from the ground after it had fallen from her hands. As he did so she could not avoid perceiving that he changed

colour very much, and then, with a troubled look
he placed the volume on the table, ardently hoping that Lizette had not been looking through
it.

" This library is not a well-chosen one," he
said, recovering his composure with an effort.
" I do not approve of many of the works in it at
all.   I was telling Lady Bend a few days ago that
it would be advisable to commit a great part of
them to the flames."

" I have only looked into one book in the room
and I must say I did not like it," said
Lizette.

" I shall try for one or two that I know you
would like," he said rising with alacrity and
looking over the volumes ranged on the surrounding shelves.   He had lighted upon one, and was
bringing it towards her with something of his
former manner, when the door was hastily opened
and Mary Pilmer looked in.

" Oh, I was not aware that you were here,
Captain Crosbie," she uttered in chilling accents ;
" excuse me, I am really sorry for having interrupted you," and giving one earnest look at
Lizette, who did not appear very distinct in the
gathering twilight, she immediately retreated,
closing the door after her in a manner not pecu-
liarly gentle.   Suddenly Dillon Crosbie's manner
changed ; he had scarcely time to say " I beg
your pardon, Miss Stutzer," and to fling the book
out of his hand so hurriedly that it fell with a
great bang to the floor, before he left the apartment in much confusion.   And was this the brave
youth who had been so cool and collected in the
midst of shipwreck and danger a few years ago,
now grown so timid and easily frightened ?
Lizette almost pitied him as much as she
assuredly would have done had she known the
real secret of his feelings.   She considered that,
perhaps, he had entangled himself in an engage-

ment with Mary Pilmer against his reason and judgment. Her beauty and wealth might have dazzled him, and led him into a snare from which he could not escape. Surely there did not seem to be much love mixed up with this constant fear of annoying the girl by the slightest mark of inattention. To her eyes it seemed that Mary was a most haughty, imperious person, exacting to the last degree—one who would be dearly purchased as a wife by any man. She got up to look over the titles of the books in the library, thinking she could easily judge by the names of the authors what the works were like, and was much shocked to perceive that many which her eye lit upon were written by well-known infidels and anti-Christian philosophers, whose names she had always heard spoken of with horror. Some were of antique date, lettered with the names of former proprietors of Darktrees, ancestors of Sir James Bend, while others seemed quite new, and had evidently been purchased by the present owner of the mansion. Lizette was very sad, for though she could not help being aware that depravity of tastes and infidel opinions existed in the world, it was still fearful to her to find herself thrown into what she might consider one of the abiding places of such dark horrors. It almost seemed as though a house containing such blasphemous works could not be safe to dwell in. And as it happened, Dark-trees was not safe to dwell in just at the present crisis.

CHAPTER X.

UNPLEASANT OCCURRENCES.

IT was quite dusky when Lizette quitted the library to dress for dinner; she did not ring for any one to assist her at her toilet, but Martha Skelton being on the watch for her, hurried to her room, and was speedily in attendance.

" You didn't walk out at all, Miss?" said Martha, as she arranged her hair.

" No, not to-day."

" Nor drive, nor anything. Dear me, but you must have spent a drearisome day, ma'am ! Mr.

Bagly, the steward, was asking for you ; he says he knew you well, ma'am."

Lizette could not help colouring at this information, but Martha did not notice it.

" He's a very nice man, ma'am ; he is indeed," continued the girl, looking with a little of the cunning of her class at Miss Stutzer's face as she spoke, trying to find out what the young lady's opinion might be, before she ventured on expressing one of her own.   " Him and the master's great entirely ; indeed Mr. Bagly is more the master, to all appearance, than Sir James."

Again Martha gave a furtive look at the young lady's face, vainly endeavouring to read its expression, but the latter was not going to commit herself by saying anything either to the advantage or disadvantage of the steward.   Full well she knew that the girl only wanted the slightest encouragement to induce her to commence pouring forth the comments of the servants at Darktrees upon all that was happening and likely to happen in the place.

"In other houses like this there would be balls and parties when visitors would be staying in it, ma'am," observed Martha, who had now arrived at fastening the young lady's. dress, " but God knows there won't be anything of that kind here ; it's more likely there will be a funeral than a ball —that's what we think below in the hall."

Lizette did not ask for an explanation of this mysterious sentence, but putting on her bracelet, and giving one pardonable glance in the mirror, hurried to the drawing-room. Here she found assembled Lady Bend, her sister, and Dillon Crosbie, and approaching the former she took her position near her, when again the conviction that she was an intruder forced itself upon her. She ardently wished that this could be the last day of such disagreeable mortifications as she had been subjected to since her arrival ; but no, she must have patience and wait till the fitting time comes for her to depart. How thankful did she now feel that she had a home to go to, even at Lonehill, and a relative to feel interested in her, to whom she could fly for shelter. Ay, even old Lonehill, with its rats and cats, and cabbage garden—its dust and rust and scanty fires would be a paradise compared to this dreadful restraint and misery in a grand old mansion where everyone wanted to get rid of her. All these thoughts passed through her mind as she sat silently beside Lady Bend, who was leaning back in an armchair near the fire, with one transparent hand placed before her face, shielding it from the blaze which gave light to the large room—shielding it, perhaps, from the gaze of curious eyes, for there were tears trembling on those pale cheeks—dropping stealthily on the rich dress that enveloped the beautiful form of the wearer.

Lizette scarcely spoke at all; indeed the silence

in the vast room was oppressive. It was a relief
when dinner was announced. Again Lady Bend
conducted Miss Stutzer from the drawing-room,
allowing her sister and Dillon Crosbie to precede
them.

"We do not make a stranger of you," whispered
Bessie, as she pressed her friend's arm; but
Lizette could make no answering pressure—she
could not even say, "Thank you; I am glad you
do not." She felt that Lady Bend's speech
savoured of hypocrisy of a clumsy kind.

At dinner Miss Stutzer sat opposite, as on the
previous day, to Miss Pilmer, and during the con-
tinuance of the repast she once or twice caught
her eye, each time being struck by a wavering,
unsteady expression in her glance which caused a
disagreeable, almost startling impression on her
mind. Was it prejudice that made her think
Mary's expression dark and unpleasant? she asked
herself the question over and over again, and

knowing as she did, how deceitful the human heart is, she could scarcely presume to answer it boldly.   Were her own eyes veiled in any way with a green shade when she looked at those exquisitely formed features?   Did she only survey them to find lurking faults, where other more honest eyes would not look for them?   She had plenty of time to think a great deal during dinner, for hardly anyone spoke while it lasted. Mary looked certainly much less sweet-tempered than she had done in the morning, and she only replied in short monosyllables when addressed by Captain Crosbie, who seemed very much at a loss to find out what to say to her, and at last took refuge in silence, which, perhaps, was the best method he could have adopted under existing circumstances.

Suddenly Lizette received a great shock.   Lady Bend fainted, and having dropped from her chair, lay motionless on the ground.   It was a curious fact that no servant ever attended at dinner at Darktrees, except while the first course was being handed round; they were dismissed then, with an order not to return unless summoned by a little bell that was generally placed beside their mistress on the table. Thus, when Lady Bend fainted, there was no one in the room at the time, besides herself, her cousin, her sister, and Miss Stutzer. Captain Crosbie arose instantly, but without any exclamation, and lifted her from the floor. Mary arose also, and although not so gentle as her cousin in rendering assistance, her plan of recovering her sister succeeded better than any other might have done. She dashed a whole carafe of water on Lady Bend's face, saying as she did so, in a tone of unconcern that surprised Lizette:

"If that does not restore her to her senses I know not what will!"

Lady Bend instantly opened her eyes; she was reclining in Crosbie's arms.

" I think I can support my sister," said Mary coldly, as she placed her arm around her. Captain Crosbie at once relinquished his burthen to her, and Lady Bend sighing heavily, gradually re-gained consciousness. Lizette by instinct, ran to her side, for there was something very touching in the expression of her features; and she was too much alarmed to remember the past, when Mary, turning round haughtily said, as if speaking to an impertinent servant :

" Do not stand so close, please ; Lady Bend requires all the air we can let her have."

Lizette retreated colouring to the eyes, and stood as ordered, in the distance; Captain Crosbie seemed very much perturbed.

" Had not your sister better go to her room ?" he ventured to suggest, speaking in a low tone to Mary. She flashed a scornful look at him without deigning any reply, and he shrank into silence at once. Lady Bend now endeavoured to stand up, and in a faint tone said she would retire from the dining-room.

"Then I shall ring for your maid," said Mary, stretching forth her hand for the little bell.

"No," said Bessie, suddenly arresting her; "I do not want any servant near me," and she withdrew, looking ghastly in the extreme. Mary followed her from the room, and when they were gone Captain Crosbie seemed very much at a loss to know how to look or what to say to the young lady remaining in his company. Lizette saw his constraint quickly enough, and having now come to the conclusion that she was not to be treated with ceremony or politeness by anyone at Darktrees except the servants, she took an early opportunity of leaving the dining-room, and withdrawing to her own apartment.

CHAPTER XI.

A MYSTERIOUS APPARITION.

THE housekeeper rapped at the door at about nine o'clock, and said Lady Bend had requested her to ascertain if she would like to have coffee in her own room, as her ladyship was unable to leave hers any more that evening. To this somewhat strange proposal Lizette replied that she certainly would prefer to sup alone, whereupon Martha Skelton was despatched to her, bearing a silver tray, upon which rested a tiny silver coffee-urn, a cup and saucer, cake, &c.

" The mistress is ill, I hear," said the girl, as she laid the tray down, with a frightened expression of countenance.

" Yes, she appears very delicate," replied Lizette.

" Poor lady, she does, and such a lovely creature as she is too; it's a mortal pity of her ; but if she had known as much as others, she never would have come to Darktrees."

" Why ?"

" Because, ma'am, it's no place for the ladies of the baronets to live. There hasn't been a Lady Bend for years that didn't die before she was twenty-five ; most of them don't live two years."

" I daresay Darktrees is not a healthy place," said Miss Stutzer.

" Well it isn't that, ma'am, altogether, though goodness knows it's as damp as the river nearly. But there's surely enchantment about the place ; and there isn't one of us below in the hall that don't believe her ladyship's under a spell of some sort ; for all within a few weeks latterly she's fading away, for all the world like a shadow. She roused herself up a little after that nice young gentleman, Captain Crosbie, that's going to marry Miss Pilmer, came down here ; but after a while she only grew worse than before.   Goodness knows we all pity her from our hearts."

Lizette feared it would be vain to endeavour to dispel Martha's notions respecting the spells hovering over her mistress ; so she held her peace on that point, pretty well convinced in her own mind that if anything was preying upon Lady Bend's spirits it was not the effect of enchantment or witchcraft.

" I suppose, ma'am, you'll stay here till Miss Pilmer's wedding takes place," resumed Martha, as she added coals to the fire.

" I did not know she was to be married soon," said Lizette faintly.

"Oh, dear, yes, ma'am; she and Captain Crosbie are to be married early next month."

And Bessie had never told her friend this !
Miss Stutzer did not know what feeling was
uppermost in her heart as she was obliged to lean
back in her chair from excess of emotion, at the
servant's words, while Martha continued, " Miss
Pilmer herself told me about the wedding taking
place almost immediately. She's a lovely, majestic
young lady; for my part I think her handsomer
than Lady Bend, though others don't. There's
Mr. Bagly—goodness me, to hear him talk of
comparing the two! But, indeed, he's a queer
man; he says such odd things, that nobody ought
to repeat. Miss Pilmer's a very generous lady; she
brought no maid here, and I attend her now and
then, though very little for that matter, as the
Mistress attends her herself like a slave. I never
saw a sister so fond of another as she is of Miss
Pilmer ; and then she's so anxious to let Captain

Crosbie and her talk together without disturbing
them.   I wouldn't mind one word Mr. Bagly
said—not I.   He's a very respectable man no
doubt, but he *does* say such odd things about
everybody!"   And thus the girl rambled on,
evidently expecting the young lady to draw her
out by questions or remarks; but Lizette was
determined she would not encourage any gossip-
ping about affairs at Darktrees.   She felt a
peculiar dislike to hear anything of Mr. Bagly's
sentiments.   So Martha was obliged to take her
departure unsatisfied with the amount of her
revelations from the servants' hall.   Lizette
drank a little coffee, and then read for a short
time, after which she commenced a letter to her
grandaunt, which served to pass away some
hours ; but determining not to sit up as late as
she had done the previous night, she undressed
before the dull clock far off had tolled out the

midnight hour, and was fast asleep in bed before one o'clock.

Something soon awoke her, she knew not how, or at what precise time ; but with pitch darkness surrounding her, she found herself lying wide awake in her bed. Fancy sometimes plays strange pranks with us ; but Lizette could scarcely attribute to imagination the decided conviction which now possessed her, that something was moving stealthily through her room, making only the shadow of a noise. It was not like the movement of a cat or rat, or any small animal ; it seemed to her as if some large being was present, treading lightly along the boards, and making great pauses of stillness between every one or two steps.   Her heart beat till its throbbing drowned all other sounds ; her eyes tried to pierce the thick gloom around her, and she thought she could discern a faint white shade of considerable extent moving nearer and nearer to the bed.   Sensation seemed now departing from her.   She wished to call out, " Who is there ?" but her tongue refused to utter the words.   The stealthy steps interrupted by the long pauses of stillness continued till they ceased altogether.   She closed her eyes unwilling to pierce the darkness any longer, and over her ice-cold face a hot breath seemed to glow. She was convinced that something was bending over her lower, and lower till her face was almost touched.   Still she lay motionless, unable to move or speak, when gradually it seemed to her as if the steps began again to rustle on the floor, and as if the being in her room was retreating farther and farther from the bed.   She soon ceased to hear any further sounds, and she was certain the room no longer contained any moving occupant save herself, though there was no audible closing or opening of the door, to let her think that her mysterious visitant had departed in an ordinary fashion. But that she was once more alone she had no doubt, all movement and shadowy noise having ceased. When all was still again, partial courage returned to her. Was all this then merely the effect of fancy? How could she believe that her imagination, however heated and overstrained, could have conjured up such a vivid conviction that something either natural or supernatural was in her room? In vain she tried to compose herself to sleep again; it was not till the first ray of morning light came struggling down the chimney and through the window-shutters, that she fell off into a sound slumber.

It was late, very late when she awoke, and no servant had been in her room with hot water, though she saw by the clock on the mantel-piece that it was past twelve o'clock!

CHAPTER XII.

A NIGHT OF SUFFERING.

" HAVE the servants learned to neglect me too?"
she thought, as she dressed and opened the shutters herself. She felt so wretched that she determined she would certainly speak to Lady Bend
that day of leaving Darktrees at once, without
waiting even for a week to elapse since her arrival
there. Armed with this resolution, she felt more
brave and free than before, and, being dressed,
hastened to the breakfast parlour. No one was
there ; the fire was dimly burning in a very

exhausted state; the newspapers arrived some hours ago, lay unopened on the table which was strewed with remnants of toast, egg-shells, ham, bread, &c., showing that breakfast had already been partaken of by the rest of the family. She was standing in the window thoughtfully when the very pompous Mrs. Polworth made her appearance.

"Good morning, ma'am," she said. "Lady Bend desires her compliments, and hopes you are very well to-day. She is still very weak herself, and prefers remaining in her room. The house has been a good deal upset this morning by that silly young woman, Martha Skelton, taking it into her head to leave it, owing to some ridiculous fancies about ghosts; she positively had the impertinence to go off before I was up, and left all her work undone, because she imagined she heard spirits moving at her end of the house last night—that end ma'am, where your room is ; I never knew anything so nonsensical and provokingly absurd in my life. I shall order breakfast immediately. As I passed your door this morning I saw it open, ma'am, and you seemed so fast asleep when I looked in that I would not have you disturbed, thinking that very likely you did not rest well in the night, so I closed the door, and desired the maids not to call you."

Mrs. Polworth then bustled away, rustling very importantly in her thick silk dress, to send in breakast.

" How did my door happen to be open this morning ? " thought Lizette, " for surely it was firmly latched when I went to bed." However she made no audible observation to Mrs. Polworth on the subject, though the fact made some impression on her, and it struck her that, perhaps, a thief might have been making a survey of her room the night before, which made her determine to see if anything had been stolen from her,

when she should have breakfasted.   As soon then
as she had partaken of a solitary, but very comfortable, repast, she repaired to her own room.
The house seemed perfectly quiet, the only person she saw was a housemaid on the corridors,
who looked at her, she fancied, with a furtive
glance of curiosity or suspicion as she passed by
to her own bedroom; arrived here, she searched
among her drawers and boxes to see if anything
had been disturbed in them during the night,
but all remained untouched—no hand seemed to
have been laid upon anything, since her own had
last arranged them.   Thus the idea of theft
abandoned her.

Feeling considerably perturbed in mind, she
wrote several copies of a note which she wished
to send to Lady Bend, informing her that she
considered it advisable to return to her aunt at
Lonehill without delay, as she must only be very
much in the way at Darktrees while she herself

was so much indisposed. She at length finished a very well-tempered little missive, expressive of her wish to depart—breathing no strain of bitterness or ill-humour, and bearing no trace of the mortified state of her own feelings. In the afternoon she rang for Mrs. Polworth, and requested her to convey the note to lady Bend, who she heard was still unwilling to leave her room. An answer was brought to her in the course of half an hour, containing these words—

"MY DEAR LIZETTE,

"I am, indeed, very ill, and I fear you will find Darktrees too dull for me to press you to remain longer than you propose. Had you been able to come here in summer you would have found things very different; but I cannot blame you for wishing to leave. At whatever hour you choose you can, of course, order the carriage to-morrow, early or late, just as it suits you.

              " Your affectionate friend,

                        " E. BEND."

" Not a word of pressure to remain," thought Lizette; " not a word of apology for the treatment I have received. It is as well; I can now set out in peace, for she does not seem to wonder in the least at my hasty determination to return to Lonehill."

She resolved that she would order the carriage very early, indeed, next morning, and she already commenced packing up her trunk, determining never again to invite herself to the house of a dear friend who had grown rich and grand. Was not her faith in the goodness of human nature, now, staggered woefully? It is such rubs as these—real or imaginary—that turn us cynics as we advance in our journey of life. When the dinner hour was approaching she felt so unwilling to meet either Captain Crosbie or Miss Pilmer that she rung the bell once more, and requested the maid who answered the summons to inform Mrs. Polworth that she did not feel inclined to appear in the dining parlour that evening, and would remain in her room for the rest of the night. Whether this announcement sounded strange or not to the damsel, who slowly retreated on hearing it, she did not particularly care, since she had now obviated the necessity of again encountering haughty looks and cold speeches, while she remained in the house, for she hoped to be on her way to Bretton-wold railway station before the customary breakfast hour next day. Dinner was sent to her in her room, and likewise coffee as on the preceding evening ; after which a message was brought to her from Lady Bend saying that she did not feel well enough to take leave of her personally, but that she hoped, if it was her intention to leave Darktrees the following morning she would have a fine day and a pleasant journey. This was a cold message enough, but Lizette had reconciled herself to expect nothing better, so she was neither agitated nor disappointed. She only wished more and more that she was far away from this inhospitable, gloomy house. She determined that she would never let her grandaunt know of the treatment she had met at Darktrees—her pride would not permit that. But would not Mrs. Bromley suspect something of the truth from this hurried return to her house? Well, she might suspect it, but, if possible, she would never be convinced of it. The night wore on—the night that was to be the last of her stay in that sombre mansion. Oh! she was glad to reflect upon that word *last*.

Among all the fancies that had crowded into her mind respecting the cause of Lady Bend's

altered manner to her; she thought it not un-
likely that Bessie, remembering what Dillon
Crosbie had written to herself respecting his
passing admiration and love for her at Markham,
now feared she might stand in her sister's way.
It was a natural conclusion for the young girl to
arrive at, yet it was not the right one. What
Lizette's feelings were in contemplating this it
is difficult to say. Women are so thoroughly
imbued with the idea that they are only to love
when beloved; that she did not dare to acknow-
ledge to her own heart how much of pain she
suffered. However true it might have been, she
dared not say to herself boldly—"All Lady
Bend's unkindness, all Mary Pilmer's impertinence would be as naught to me, only that somebody else in the house is altered towards me."
Oh, no, she could not say that even in the
faintest whisper. She blushed at the very
thought of it.

When it was time to go to bed, she began to
think of the strange circumstance of her door,
which had been carefully latched the night before, having been found open that morning; and
as the hours passed by she became rather nervous,
finally going towards the door, and locking it before getting into bed.

Lady Bend sat up very late that night in her
dressing room. She had blistered and blotted
many a page of a book, and many a sheet of
paper with hot tears. Yes, and she had been on
her knees more than once within a short space of
time—on her knees, but uttering no prayer in
words, for Bessie had rarely prayed in her life,
and now her casting herself in the attitude of
worship and humility was merely an instinctive
movement—natural in a moment of despair and
helplessness. She may have cried, "God have
mercy upon me," over and over again ; the words
may have risen to her lips, but farther than that

she asked nothing of the Great Ruler. She had never communed with God in hours of happiness and ease, and now she found it hard to address Him.

When the house was still that night, and all the inmates retired to their sleeping rooms, Lady Bend was yet wakeful, without the thought of repose crossing her mind; often she came out upon the corridors, listening, with an expression of awe and terror on her countenance—starting at the click of the clock, or the creaking of the glass dome overhead, as the wind moved it—nervously watching and listening, and once even walking as far as a chamber door that was fast closed for the night. Here she stopped cautiously for a few moments, trying if she could ascertain if the occupant within had gone to rest. All was silent; there seemed to be no light within. Softly she went back to her own apartment, and then sighing heavily, closed her door.

No wonder Lady Bend looked wan and worn. No wonder there were silver streaks already mingling with her beautiful dark locks—silver hairs at twenty-two! Ay, and many of them —not one here and there, as in some heads at that early age—but many of them—congregating daily—clustering thicker and thicker after each night of grief and despair.

Again and again out upon the corridors, watching and listening. But it is long past midnight and the house is still silent. Will it remain so all night?

CHAPTER XIII.

THE MYSTERY CONTINUES.

LIZETTE slept, and fantastic dreams haunted her pillow—dreams of death and murder—of dark deeds done in former days within the walls of Sir James Bend's ancestral home; and then it seemed to her that somebody had accused herself of crime—that she was condemned to be hung. She stood on the gallows, a rope round her neck. Tighter—tighter—tighter it pressed upon her throat! tighter — tighter! Suffocation — not imaginary but real. She awoke. Great horror!

there was no fancy deceiving her now; it was no dream. She was really suffocating—choking—a hand was upon her throat—somebody was murdering her!

She opened her eyes—a pale shadowy light filled the room—gray and cold; but it revealed the dim outline of a white figure bending over her. Cold perspiration stood upon the young girl's brow. She was palsied. The hand was lifted from her throat, and a voice murmured faintly the words, "She is dead at last." With the instinct taught by despair, Lizette now felt her only safety would consist in lying perfectly still as if dead. She stretched her limbs, and scarcely allowed her breathing to be preceptible. The strong pressure of the hand that had grasped her throat, told her too plainly that her feeble strength would be no match for her antagonist, even if the latter possessed no weapon. This fearful visitant appeared endowed with great power. The moonlight shining through her open window, together with the night breeze blowing into her chamber, convinced her that the mysterious person, whoever it might be, had entered her room by the window, which could be reached and opened, no doubt from the balcony outside. Moving from the bed, the terrible being noiselessly crossed the apartment, and took up its position near the fireplace, where it occupied the antique arm-chair. Gradually growing accustomed to the moonlight, and being able to see through the division of the curtains at the foot of the bed, Lizette now watched the appearance of her fearful enemy. In the dim light it looked spectral and unearthly, the dark hair hung in masses over its shoulders, but all was so indistinct that she could discern nothing clearly. Could it be all a dream? No. She was convinced she lay wide awake. Surely she would tell Lady Bend in the morning before she left the house (if she was spared to leave it), that there was some unsafe person haunting Darktrees. The idea of it being anything supernatural never held place for a minute in her mind. It might be some of the servants playing a horrible trick —it might be a case of dangerous sleep-walking —it might be something worse still; but whatever it was, she would surely speak of it to Lady Bend before quitting the place in the morning.

It seemed wonderful to her that she did not faint under the heavy weight of fear that oppressed her; but her senses never forsook her though for a full hour that awful being sat there within her view, motionless as a carved image, or a corpse. At last it arose softly, and once more approached the bed. It placed a cold hand upon Lizette's face, and then bending down listened for the faintest sound of breathing. Lizette held her breath in till well-nigh exhausted; but her *ruse* succeeded. The would-be murderer seemed satisfied; and gliding to the door, unlocked it cautiously, and disappeared. Jumping out of bed, Lizette now locked her door again, and hastening to the window, which was wide open, closed it, fastening it down, so that it could not be opened again from without. Trembling all the while, like one paralysed, the young girl bravely performed these tasks; but her nerves had received a powerful shock. It was with difficulty she could collect her senses. She was lying in her bed wide awake, and still trembling, when she thought her ear caught the sound of sobbing and moaning, at first seeming indistinct, but gradually approaching nearer, as steps were heard coming along the corridor outside. Three distinct knocks were struck against her door, and a voice called in low tones, "Lizette, Lizette! oh, speak to me!" But fearful of betraying herself to her enemy, the young girl held her peace. Again the voice implored, "Lizette, Lizette! oh, speak to me!" but Lizette was immovable; then there was a moan—a stifled sob—very piteous to hear, and the voice called out no more. Unable to rest in her bed Lizette now got up, and dressed herself by the light of the moon. She had scarcely performed this task when the sounds of steps hurrying along the corridor towards her room again struck upon her frightened ears. There were whisperings—subdued exclamations, and a man's voice enjoining patience—silence—speaking words of hope and comfort. Great heaven! Lizette heard her door attacked vigorously—some one was forcing it open! Where could she fly to? The thought of the window rushed into her mind, and she was running towards it, when, with a strong effort, without much noise, her door sprung open. She saw lights. She saw two figures before her that made her doubt the evidence of her senses.   One was that of Lady Bend—the other that of Dillon Crosbie!

" My dearest Lizette!" exclaimed Lady Bend, rushing forward and clasping her in her arms. " Thank God you are unhurt!"

In the next instant Lizette had fainted. Restoratives were procured noiselessly from the lower part of the house; but no servant was called up.   All was done quietly.   And then when the young girl was restored to conscious- ness, Lady Bend confided to her what, alas ! could not well be kept secret from her any longer, though she was requested not to speak of the matter to any one else.   Lizette was nor sur- prised.   She had more than once during the past night guessed the truth, which had only become known to Lady Bend within the last few weeks.

CHAPTER XIV.

THE MYSTERY EXPLAINED.

MARY PILMER was insane. Naturally haughty
and overbearing, she had grown up, under the
care of Mrs. Devenish, self-willed and vain in the
extreme. Her godmother had fostered every
whim, gratified every wish of her childhood,
never constraining her to curb ill-humours, or
check a tendency she had to brood morbidly
over every imaginary cause of offence. Never
taught to submit to any authority, or to regard
herself humbly, hearing her own praises for

talents and beauty, seeing herself waited upon by obsequious domestics, and idolized by her weak, ignorant godmother, the proud girl grew up with the idea that she was a creature of a superior order to common mortals.   Eccentric since early childhood, she, however, betrayed no sign of actual derangement of intellect till the sudden death of Mrs. Devenish, which upset her reason palpably.   Captain Crosbie happened to be staying at the time at Wormley Hall, and after the funeral she expressed her wish to him of visiting her sister at Darktrees, because she understood that he was going there, for she had taken a fancy to her Cousin Dillon, and was determined to accompany him wherever he might go.   Captain Crosbie, unaware that she was labouring under any delusion, agreed at once to escort her to Darktrees, and Lady Bend wrote an affectionate letter, inviting Mary to make her house a home for the present.   Accordingly, they

set out for Darktrees, and it was only after a
time that both Crosbie and Lady Bend became
aware that Mary was deranged.   Gradually the
sad truth revealed itself. She spoke to them in
confidence of her strange delusions, one of the
most remarkable of which was, that she was the
affianced wife of her cousin Dillon.   To careless
observers she appeared perfectly sane, and hoping
that she was merely labouring under a temporary
fit of derangement, caused by the excitement
consequent on her godmother's awful and unexpected death, both Dillon and her sister wished
to preserve the matter a secret, every day looking
forward to her recovery.   Nevertheless Lady
Bend experienced much grief, as she listened to
Mary's extraordinary hallucinations, and in particular her uneasiness increased when Lizette
Stutzer arrived at Darktrees, as Mary appeared
much worse then.   She detested Miss Stutzer,
Bessie having informed her long since that

Dillon Crosbie had fallen in love with her at Markham, and she had not forgotten the intelligence. She regarded Lizette with the bitterest feelings of jealousy. Fearful of rousing or contradicting her in the least degree, both Dillon and Bessie gratified her wildest wishes, and the former paid her unwearying attention, taking care not to let her see that he took any note whatever of Lizette's presence.

"Each day, my dear Lizette," said Bessie, "I hoped that my poor sister would return to her senses, and both Dillon and I did all in our power to keep her mind perfectly calm, never irritating her in the smallest matter. Never before did I so perfectly understand the untiring kindness of my cousin as I do now. He has been unwearied in his efforts to keep my mind at ease respecting Mary, acting for the last fortnight as a regular attendant, driving her out whenever she pleased, and devoting all his time to her.   Unfortunately this attention on his part has confirmed her, perhaps, in her delusion that she is to be his wife.   There was one thing we may have been too careful of, and that was letting her discover that she was watched, or suspected of being insane, for she seemed to possess an extraordinary intuition, almost like magic, with regard to our thoughts about herself, even when we were most cautious not to let her observe that we thought her at all eccentric.   So great was our caution on this point, that though we were aware she had a fancy for sitting up late at night, we dared not attempt to let her know that any one sat up also. From sundry hints that she dropped yesterday and the day before, I dreaded that she might contemplate doing you some mischief, and for the last two nights I sat up myself, never closing an eye, yet she baffled my watchfulness, for it seems she has been in the habit of leaving her room by the window, instead of by the door, and entering other parts of the house, through such of the windows as the negligence of the servants left unsecured. In this way she entered your room. Imagine my despair, when she rushed into my room a short time ago, and told me she had strangled you! My dear Lizette, I have been sadly to blame for not revealing all this to you before. What mischief might have been caused by my folly; yet I considered the secret was one that concerned her, not myself. Dreading to behold the result of her murderous attempt, yet hoping you still might live, I hurried to your door, and called to you, but you returned no answer; then I ran to awake Dillon Crosbie, who was soon able to render me assistance. My poor sister retired quietly to her bed, and is now asleep. We forced your door open, and, thank God, you were safe. Lizette, among all the misfortunes that overwhelm me, I never could have borne another greater than them all !"

As Lady Bend uttered this last sentence, she clasped her worn hands together, with a movement that spoke of despair. Surely her sister's state of mind, afflicting as it may have been, was not enough to render this young woman so wretched, so heartbroken as she appeared.

" My dear Bessie, I sympathise with you from my heart," said Lizette, looking with pity at her friend's ghastly countenance. " How I wish I had not come at such a time to Darktrees !"

" Nay, it is as well things have happened so," returned Bessie. " All has been so far fortunate, and to-morrow my sister will leave this, under the care of my cousin and Luke Bagly."

" Luke Bagly !" repeated Lizette, in some surprise ; " and you trust that man with the secret !"

" Yes ; he is devoted to my interests, Lizette.

I know it, though I am also aware that he is a bad man."

"Then do not trust him, Bessie—take my advice. If you know him to be a bad man do not confide any secret to his keeping."

"He has already more than that in his power," murmured Lady Bend, bitterly.

Lizette met a fixed thoughtful look from her friend's eye—a look that seemed to say, "I may as well tell you all the miserable secrets that weigh upon my soul." But Bessie checked the impulse that had seized her. No, she could not confess any more at present. She only took Lizette's hand, and clasping it warmly in both her own, said:

"Oh, thank God! my dear, dear friend, that fate, hard as it seems to have been towards you, has spared you the evils that have befallen me, in spite of wealth, in spite of all that seemed to render me fortunate—the envied of many short-sighted mortals. Lizette, I stand before you here, more to be pitied, more to be despised, than the lowest kitchen-maid in this house!"

Strange words! Lizette's cheek grew paler than it had even been before. She dared not question Bessie any farther.

.

CHAPTER XV.

SIR JAMES BEND.

LUKE BAGLY, in his own way, was really attached to Lady Bend, and for her sake he pretended to be devoted to Sir James, whom he soon learned to detest. Among the many dependents of Mrs. Meiklam who loved the beautiful young lady, so often staying for days together at the Rest, Luke stood foremost. The very contrariety of their natures may have led to this attachment on his side. The straightforward, noble character of the much-spoiled girl impressed this deceitful,

cowardly man, with a peculiar admiration. If
anyone vexed Miss Bessie Pilmer, he or she
would soon be made aware of the fact.   She
never disguised her feelings on any subject, and
so her truthfulness, her courage, gained her many
friends among those whose dependent position
rendered them cunning and underhand themselves.
Now, therefore, when Bagly took up his station
as steward at Darktrees, he soon wormed himself
into the secrets of his master, for Sir James, like
all bad people, had numberless mysteries surrounding him, one leading to several.   It was
natural to think that Luke would feel more interested in the person whom he had known from
her childhood, than in him who was a stranger
till a few months back.   Few people at Darktrees, or in its neighbourhood, liked Sir James.
He was a careless landlord, seldom residing on
his property—well known to have been plunged
in great difficulties when he proposed for a

wealthy heiress in London.   There was a curious
but faint rumour afloat round Darktrees, which
Lady Bend would surely be the last person to
hear.   However, Luke Bagly heard it ; and, with
all the sagacity of his nature, he determined to
discover if there was the smallest foundation for
it.   Bad as he was himself, he was, yet, shocked
at the idea of crime and wickedness in another.
Strange as it may appear, Bagly was a kind
husband and father;   he was, therefore, not
inclined to be lenient to any one sinning on that
head, especially when the person chiefly sinned
against was a favourite of his own.   While he
thought the negociations respecting the marriage
of Miss Pilmer were not yet completed, he summoned up his courage to write a confidential
letter to that young lady from Darktrees, where,
it may be remembered, he was employed to act
as steward long before Sir James married ; but,
unhappily, the letter only reached Bessie when

she returned to England from her long wedding tour on the Continent; it had miscarried, and wandered very far indeed before arriving at its destination, having been often re-directed to foreign towns, which she and Sir James had always left before it could catch them. It would have been as well if it had never reached the owner. Too late to be of any use, it only plunged Bessie into a fearful state of mind, which lasted for a considerable length of time, when, at length she began to hope that Bagly had been misinformed, that the statement he had made was altogether false. She was determined not to believe it. All that spring she plunged into wild gaiety, beginning the life she had married to lead. No one was more admired in London that season than the wealthy Lady Bend; her dresses were exquisite, her beauty dazzling, but her heart cankering all the while. Her father's last words, spoken on his death-bed, were always

coming up to her mind, and the more she thought
of them, the more she danced and dressed, and
sought excitement in ball-rooms.   Then came a
hint from Sir James that all this gaiety must
cease; he could not afford to keep up an establishment in London !   He wanted all the ready
money he could muster up to pay debts of his
own—debts of his father's also.   Oh, the dark
array of creditors he had !   Darktrees must be
sold unless they were satisfied at once.   Sir
James quarrelled with his mother-in-law, who
had tried so ardently to get him for her daughter's
husband.   Well, there was no love lost between
them, for Mrs. Pilmer had only valued him for
his title.   The Baronet told her this and much
more; he said what never could be forgotten or
forgiven, and Mrs. Pilmer swore most vehemently
that she would never set foot within the walls of
Darktrees Hall; upon which Sir James politely
told her that nobody wanted her to go there. Oh,

the insolence—the wickedness—the cruelty ex-
hibited by this most paltry of tyrants ! What
Bessie endured from him, none but herself knew
—none would ever know—not even her own
mother.

On leaving London and arriving at Darktrees,
Bessie experienced much despondency of mind;
and, influenced either by a desire to make mischief, or by mistaken kindness, Luke Bagly dared
to poison her mind with the most fearful insinua-
tions.   She listened with ill-feigned indignation
and contempt ; her white lips and trembling frame
contradicting but too powerfully what her words
betokened.   Bagly knew she more than half believed his words : then he had his own character
to vindicate ; and perhaps, he wished to gratify
his love of power ; and he spied, and wormed out
secrets till he was convinced of the truth of his
assertions.   *He believed Sir James Bend to be*
guilty of a great crime.   He pitied the unfortunate

young lady who had been ensnared into putting herself in the power of such a man; for her sake his lips remained closed upon the matter to all except herself.   Some evil spirit prompted him to tell her all he knew.   There were unmistakable proofs of Sir James Bend's guilt.   Perhaps this man had grown hardened since, in his early youth he stood trembling before judge and jury in a public court, to answer for the part he had taken in a young comrade's murder.   Never had he forgotten that frightful evening, when the victim of his ferocious temper lay slain before his eyes; never had he forgotten the day when, before the unpitying gaze of scores of curious men, he stood accused of that awful crime.   It was all past now ; but if he stood again in a court of justice, awaiting the decision of a jury in a matter that concerned his own life or death, or transportation for unknown years, he never more could experience over again the same tension of nerves—the same degree of horror

unspeakable.   There were few good points in Sir
James Bend's character; but he had never been
utterly devoid of feeling for *himself*.   From the day
he was acquitted of all intent to seriously injure his
slain companion, he felt that he was blasted.   It
was not sorrow for having caused the death of an
unoffending lad, the only son of his mother, and
she was a widow, or for having ruined his unfortunate schoolmaster—that preyed upon him—
but a kind of hatred of mankind in general.
Instead of being humbled, he only grew moody
and worse tempered than ever; he plunged into
dissipation, dwelt much abroad, gambled, held
companionship with desperate and unprincipled
men; his title and estates had descended to him
incumbered by fearful debts, incurred by his
father and grandfather; he had great liabilities of
his own also—he was hampered woefully on all
sides.   Do not think we mean to excuse him for
any guilty plan he may have resolved upon to

extricate himself from difficulties ; we are only stating facts. He was tempted, as all have been tempted since Satan crept among mankind, and he yielded to the voice of the tempter, as, thank God, all do *not* yield.

CHAPTER XVI.

STRANGE COMMUNICATIONS.

LADY BEND requested Lizette Stutzer to remain
for some time longer at Darktrees; and as the
latter now understood why it was that her presence
there had seemed so unwelcome up to this time,
she consented to do so. As had been arranged,
Mary Pilmer was induced to leave the house under
the escort of her cousin, Dillon Crosbie; and,
yielding to Lizette's advice, Bessie did not confide
anything respecting her sister's mental state to
any domestic at Darktrees, including the very

acute Luke Bagly, who, to say the truth, had already some suspicions that Miss Pilmer was not altogether of sound intellect; but he had no particular wish to learn anything positive about the matter. It was not in his line, and did not concern him. It was enough for him, at present, that Lady Bend herself was much in his power, and Sir James, too, for that matter. Mary Pilmer and Dillon Crosbie set off at once for London, where the young lady was handed over to the care of her afflicted mother, already suffering severely from her son-in-law's barbarous incivility, and pining for the company of her dearly loved Bessie, whom she would not venture to visit at Darktrees after the solemn vow she had made never to set foot within its walls.

Thus Lizette and her dear friend were alone at the sombre mansion of Darktrees Hall; but the former soon discovered that Lady Bend was suffering from some secret cause of grief which prevented them being on confidential terms. Nothing could exceed the kindness of her hostess, nor the attention of the servants; yet there was a dullness hanging over the whole house most depressing.   Bessie seldom spoke of her husband : she neither blamed nor praised him.   Soon he would be nothing to her—she nothing to him— that was her chief thought.   Sometimes she drove out accompanied by Lizette, but she never went to church on Sundays.   This was a grief to her pious young friend.

" Shall we read the Bible to-day?" asked Miss Stutzer, one Sunday afternoon as they sat together.

" No, thank you," replied Bessie hastily, and colouring a little.

" Oh, Bessie, why not?" asked Lizette, in much sorrow.   " Surely you can have no serious objection ?"

" If you wish to read for yourself I will leave

you," was Lady Bend's response; and in the next moment she had left the room.

The Bible had never been a favourite book of Bessie's—now it was less so than ever; it was regarded as decidedly inimical to her present views, for this unfortunate young woman was contemplating a fearful crime—she was about to place herself on a par with the very lost and degraded —the most unpardonable of guilty sinners.

Sir James Bend, unaware that Luke Bagly felt any particular interest in his mistress, and knowing him to be a man of great sagacity and cunning, at the same time that he was one of low principles, had gradually taken him into his confidence more than was altogether prudent. Through these means Bagly had become possessed of the secret which so fatally concerned both the Baronet and his new bride. Luke had never been scrupulous in the matter of opening and reading the letters of his employers—thus gathering all the information respecting their affairs that was essential to gratify his curiosity; and whatever Sir James felt it judicious to withhold from his knowledge, he learned by underhand and unlawful proceedings. He was playing at the same time the part of spy and traitor towards two guilty beings, while he was really attached to another whom he pitied as much as it was in his nature to pity any human creature. To serve this latter unfortunate individual Bagly would have staked a great deal; he could be desperate when he chose—ay, even in the cause of *somebody else*. Then he loved the law still as much as ever; and this would be a grand case for prosecution and punishment. How he would have loved to bring on a public trial, for the edification of half the civilized world, only for the sake of one of the parties concerned, who would be sorely compromised by the proceeding!

One particular post brought Bagly two remarkable letters. One contained these words :—

" LUKE BAGLY,

" What you say astonishes me much.   Do
not believe a word of what that woman asserts; she
has not the slightest foundation for what she has
told you.   No doubt she would be delighted to
injure me if she could—either by fair means or
false.   She would, of course, try any method of
revenge, however absurd.   She must be put to
silence—that is all.   If she writes to you again
let me know at once.

" JAMES BEND."

The other epistle ran as follows :—

" DEAR SIR,

" I am most thankful for your friendly advice.
When I partially consented to the arrangement
which Sir James proposed to me as the only safe
and certain way of rescuing him from ruin, I
never thought of the consequences that might

ensue to myself. I have been much to blame in
the whole proceedings. Threats—tortures should
never have induced me to listen to such an
iniquitous proposal. But there was beggary—
starvation staring me in the face; and not alone
me, but others dearer to me than myself. Oh, I
pity that poor lady at Darktrees—God have mercy
on her! My own health is precarious; life will
soon cease to be a burden to me: but not for
myself alone do I want justice—I do not deserve
it; but those whom I will leave behind me must
not be sacrificed; whatever I may have done to
forfeit all pity—all mercy from the world, *my sons
must and shall have their rights.* Their father
need not think he can blast them for any base
purpose. I will rise up yet before I die and pro-
claim his and my own iniquity before the face of
all people, to save my sons from a worse ignominy
than even their parents' guilt can brand them
with. My marriage certificate, which you kindly

say I should secure a copy of, is registered in the books of the parish church of Holme-Regis in ——shire, the date of it being 10th April, 18—, more than six years ago."

This letter bore a foreign postmark, but no signature, and was addressed to " Luke Bagly, Esq." for Luke, in writing to the person from whom it came, had represented himself to be a person connected with the law, who in some mysterious manner had become aware of facts by no means concerning himself, and in which he was interested merely for the sake of justice. This correspondence was strictly private and confidential.

Without stating where he was going, Luke set off by railway from Bretton-wold one fine autumn morning, and travelled in the direction of the very unimportant village of Holme-Regis.

.

CHAPTER XVII.

THE POISON.

IT was late at night; Lady Bend was sitting by the library fire; Lizette was gone to bed; the house was generally quiet; but the mistress of Darktrees was not alone. Luke Bagly stood before her, arguing, demonstrating, threatening, in his ardour to serve her.

"Look here, ma'am," he said, striking his hands together, "with one blaze of the fire I could destroy all proof of that marriage. I tore the certificate out of the register while the sexton was shutting the vestry door, and I have it in my pocket here. That woman and her brats wouldn't have the value of a straw to go upon if I'd burn that piece of paper." And the poor scrawled memorandum of that true and legal marriage wavered in Bessie's eyesight.

" Do not attempt to destroy it !" she exclaimed firmly, adding in a quieter tone, "I thank you, Bagly, for your wish to serve me ; however wrong your intentions may be, but I am fully determined to commit no act of injustice towards others. I have been blighted myself—that is enough."

" Then as God is looking down on us both this night, I'll make that villain suffer !" exclaimed the steward, thrusting the certificate once more into his pocket. " I'll never stand by and see the honourable and the innocent ruined in this way !'

" Listen, Bagly ; as you value my peace here

and hereafter, let this matter rest quietly. To act otherwise would be to plunge me into greater misery than I suffer even now. My own mother, my dearest friend, will never learn from my lips the miserable position I stand in."

"And this is your wish, my lady ?"

"Most certainly it is."

"You will seek no revenge—no redress ?"

"Never."

"And you will live on here as if nothing was wrong ?"

Lady Bend did not reply. She had made up her mind as to the course she would pursue, but she did not choose to reveal it at present.

"Bagly, will you take an oath for me here now ?" she asked, suddenly.

"If I can I will, most surely, ma'am," was the man's reply, as he gazed with a sort of awe upon the still lovely, though sadly altered face of the unfortunate lady before him.

" Swear, then, most solemnly, that from this night you will never utter a word to mortal about this most wretched business; that as long as you live you will keep it secret from the whole world."

"But why should I swear that?" he asked, his eyes twinkling maliciously. "Why should I allow a wretch like Sir James to escape punishment?"

"You have a family, Luke," continued Lady Bend; "money would serve them; a thousand pounds will be transferred to your account here, on the spot, if you swear what I ask; and also if you deliver up to me that register of marriage from your pocket."

Bagly looked doubtingly for a minute or so at the lady's countenance. Right well, however, his keen observation told him that she meant to act no underhand part. He dared not tell her that he was already in league with her own mother respecting an iniquitous business, and he knew she was perfectly unaware of it.

" Excuse me, ma'am," he said, after a pause ; " but what good would my taking that oath do you? I might close my lips upon this terrible misfortune, but would others be equally silent? I might, of course, take your money, and swear what you wish, yet you would find yourself still in danger. That woman in Paris will speak out without delay. She has threatened as much."

" Leave all the rest to me, Bagly ; all I require of you is this oath, that register of marriage, and a promise that you will instantly leave Dark-trees, and never hold communion with any of its inmates after your departure."

" And yourself, madam ? Do you imagine that, bad as I may appear, I would leave this place with my mind at ease, careless of what might become of you? No, ma'am ; you mistake me if you hold that opinion."

"As to me, Bagly, you need suffer no uneasiness. Rest assured that I know what I am about. I want no revenge—nothing but silence from you while I live, and after I am dead. I wish solely for peace. Will you take the oath and the reward?"

Lady Bend arose to get a pen and ink, and as she did so, a small phial dropped from her lap where it had rested. Bagly stooped to pick it up from the spot near his foot where it had rolled. He gave one of his quick glances at the label round it, and then, without betraying the slightest change of countenance, placed it carelessly on the mantel-piece. The lady watched him as he did so, somewhat anxiously, and then drew the writing materials near to her.

"Stay, madam," said Bagly; "do not write anything now; to-morrow will do better to make any arrangement than now in the dead of night. I'll sleep over your proposal."

"Nay, Luke, I cannot delay this matter. If you do not agree at once to take the oath and deliver up to me that marriage register, you will never have the opportunity of doing so again."

"If you would let me fling that odious paper into the fire there, I'd do it willingly, ma'am," he replied, approaching the grate with a sudden movement, and in some unaccountable manner knocking the small phial from the mantel-piece with his arm. It fell on the fender, and broke into fragments. Lady Bend rushed forward with a cry. In that destruction she saw the ruin of all that she had at this time to hope for.

"It's no great mischief I've done, anyway," said Bagly, stooping low to push the pieces of shattered glass farther under the grate, "for I believe it was only poison was in the bottle."

"Stay," shrieked Lady Bend, as Bagly stooped over the fender, where the subtle and deadly fluid was lying in a fearful pool; "you are imprudent to go near it!"

The words were spoken too late; that most frightful of poisons—the swiftest, subtlest of all noxious death-fluids—had done its work.   The deadly vapour stole insidiously upwards; Bagly staggered—stared wildly, ferociously round him. Was it possible that this was the feeling of coming death?   Then giddiness—stupor—vain to endeavour to shake it off.   He shook like some great forest animal suddenly struck with a fatal blow.   To save her, he had killed himself unwittingly!   Ay, in that moment of horror, the thought occurred to him.

With her hands clasped, Lady Bend watched, as in a dream, this frightful termination of that midnight consultation; and then, rousing herself, she ran to the assistance of the wretched steward.   He was now struggling, and insensible on the floor—his features contorted—his hands clenched—his colour rapidly changing to a fearful cadaverous hue.   This was the death she had believed would have been easy !   Terror-stricken the unfortunate young woman did not lose her presence of mind.   Hastily securing the paper which Bagly had dropped from his hand when suddenly seized with vertigo, she hurried from the room and alarmed the servants.   The house was soon astir; the little pool on the library fender had dried up in the heat of the fire; the tiny glass fragments mingled with ashes and cinders; no one sought for the cause of this awful and mysterious death beneath the grate of that sombre room.   Perhaps Mr. Bagly had been drinking hard; perhaps it was an attack of heart disease.   The apothecary from the village did not know—or did not care particularly—what was the cause of death, but set it down as heart disease, which he considered to be a convenient cause of sudden death.   The most wonderful part of the matter was, what the steward was doing in the library at that hour; but there was no coroner's inquest. Some of the servants had seen the man alive in the last agonies of death; and the mistress had been in the very room when he staggered and fell; and had called them up. It was all wonder, confusion, and comment. Her ladyship was in her bed, too ill to be annoyed with questions of an exciting nature. It would be well to get the dead man coffined and buried as soon as possible. To tell the truth, Luke Bagly had not been liked at Darktrees among the servants there; and no one wept at his funeral. His death was an awful warning— nothing more. An awful warning indeed! A warning to the lady lying so motionless and weak in the velvet-curtained bed, in the grandest chamber of that grand old mansion, so remote from London detectives or even common provincial police. Ah, there are a great deal of

wonderful things done in the world that nobody
hears about through the newspapers, glad as those
inquisitive organs of public information would
be to penetrate all mysteries, and lay bare all
family secrets.   What was going on at Darktrees
Hall at that time never went beyond the old-
fashioned village—scarcely beyond the demesne
gates.   There was talk about ghosts, and gossip
about the Bends' hereditary wickedness generally,
and rumours of improbable doings; and sometimes the truth was hit upon, though so encompassed round about with lies and false reports
that no one knew where it stood.   One conviction
possessed the minds unanimously of all the
lower servants at the Hall, and that was, that
the Baronet's wife was fast sinking under the
fatal spell that had always proved so disastrous
to the ladies of Darktrees.

Lady Bend was really seriously ill—mentally
and bodily.   Lizette Stutzer was still her devoted

friend, watching day after day, ay, and night after night, beside her couch.   Humbled more by the experience she had had of that fearful death by a sudden, subtle poison—occurring before her eyes, like a testimony and a warning—than by all the woeful wretchedness that had hitherto been her lot to bear, Lady Bend learned to thank God that Providence had spared her from committing the fearful crime of self-murder.   Never more would she raise her hand against her own life; but she would pray to be taken away, whenever it might please her Father, from despair and disgrace.   Night and day that was her prayer.

CHAPTER XVIII.

THE LOST FOUND.

MANY strange occurrences often happen to the same people at the same time, or with reference to them. Scarcely had Mrs. Pilmer heard of the death of Luke Bagly, which relieved her of a great weight of uneasiness, than some unlooked for information from Mr. Hill, the attorney at Yaxley, reached her—proving to her that she had indeed been duped by that cunning man, no longer living. Hill had been put lately in possession of Mrs. Meiklam's lost will in a strange way. It appeared that one of the poachers, who so often frequented the grounds of the Rest, had found it, the very night Bagly had dropped it from his pocket, and attaching little importance to it had conveyed it from the spot. Some of his companions, more learned than himself, soon discovered that this simple sheet of paper, folded up like a letter, was nothing less than the will of the great lady at the Rest, who so suddenly died at the same time. These men all thoroughly detested Bagly; and seeing his name noted down in the document for what seemed to them an extraordinary legacy of one hundred pounds, they determined not to deliver up the will, hoping thereby to do the hateful steward an injury. Fearful of committing the crime of destroying it, the man who found it hid it carefully in the bottom of a chest in his cottage, thinking that a time might arrive when he could gain some advantage by the production of it.

Meanwhile Bagly, having over and over again read the will, and copied it from time to time during Mrs. Meiklam's lifetime, was now fully competent to write a pretty correct transcript of it from memory; and trusting to impose on Mrs. Pilmer after her husband's death, he tried his skill at a *ruse*, which succeeded well.   Duped by the legal terms of the document which Luke submitted to her perusal, the lady felt that it possibly *might* be a copy of the original will in his possession, and fearful of sifting the matter any further, she consented to give him an annual sum of money, together with a promise of pro-curing him an engagement as steward at Dark-trees, on condition that she should hear no more about the affair.   This was all he wanted or could expect.   After all it was soothing to him to reflect that his nightly attempts of forgery had at length been turned to good account.   Often Mrs. Pilmer felt on the point of breaking off this secret league with Bagly; it was repugnant to her feelings in every way; she was not a kind woman, nor a downright honest one, but she was not palpably wicked enough for any great crime. Her conscience was uneasy; not because she feared detection, but because she comprehended that she was laying herself open to a frightful accusation of guilt. When the tidings of Bagly's sudden death reached her, we must say she felt very little regret, rather the reverse; but neither was she greatly grieved when a letter arrived at Markham House from Hill the attorney at Yaxley, scarcely a week after the news of Luke's death, stating that David Jobling, labourer in the vicinity of Meiklam's Rest, had just handed to him the will he had last made for Mrs. Meiklam, which the said David declared had been found by him on the grounds of Meiklam's Rest some time since, though he was not aware of its importance at the time of discovery, &c., &c.

As no one could possibly conceive what Jobling's reasons might be for hitherto concealing a document by no means concerning himself, one way or another, there was not much questioning about the matter. The will was there—uninjured —palpably in John Hill's well-known writing, and signed by Grace Meiklam with unmistakable clearness. The people at Yaxley had heard Luke Bagly was dead, and that was why Jobling produced the will; but he gained nothing from Mr. Hill for his pains, though that gentleman would come in for fifty pounds by way of remembrance from the deceased lady of the Rest. However Jobling did not despair. Captain Crosbie or Miss Stutzer would surely reward him for restoring them to their rights, for the former was to be master of all the lands attached to Meiklam's Rest, and the latter to receive a legacy of seven thousand pounds.

What a stir all this made at Yaxley and in its

neighbourhood! How everybody talked and raved; but no one was more rejoiced and excited than old Jenny Black; she clapped her hands, laughed, and prophesied wondrous things. Didn't she know all along that Miss Lizette would be rich and grand, and that Master Crosbie would be a great gentleman? Master Crosbie happened to be in Ireland at that time, business having called him there. Good-luck seemed to have taken a sudden turn in his favour. Riches were pouring on him in unexpected profusion. But what confusion might not Mrs. Pilmer be plunged in now, had her nephew chosen to be disagreeable! How much money she would have to refund to him—money taken up long since and spent by herself, or handed over to Sir James Bend to pay his debts! But Dillon Crosbie did not choose to be disagreeable or exacting; whatever of ready money, lawfully due to himself.

had been spent by the Pilmers need not be returned to him. He would never distress his uncle's
family—never put to the slightest inconvenience
his Cousin Bessie or her husband. Could he
forget that his early years were all passed under
his uncle's roof—that he owed his education, his
profession to him? Could he forget that
his dear cousin, Lady Bend, had promised
him assistance, in a pecuniary point of view, when
she thought he might need it? No—his memory
would never fail him on these scores; all those
thousands swallowed up in the gulf of debt
and extravagance might remain unheard of
evermore.

It was now very late in the winter, quite on
the borders of spring, but Lizette was still with
her friend at Darktrees. Sir James Bend had
been all the autumn and winter away—in Scotland first, then at Paris, or in Italy. Lizette

could not help remarking that his wife never, by
any chance, alluded to him of herself; and
seemed always anxious to change the subject
when asked about him.

CHAPTER XIX.

MEIKLAM'S REST.

WITH a pale face and trembling frame, Sir James
Bend read the following letter, addressed to him
at his club in London :—

"I know all now; further disguise or secrecy
can avail nothing as far as I am concerned; but
for the sake of those who are near and dear to
me, I will let matters rest quietly. Your fate
lies in the hollow of my hand; if I wished I
could ruin you—brand you as the most wretched

of criminals before the whole world; while, on the other hand, I could destroy all proof of your guilt, and of my own most miserable position; but not even to save myself from the disgrace and pity that I so much dread, would I dare to commit such an act of injustice.   All I ask, now, of you is, that you dispose of Darktrees at once, and leave England—the whole British dominions in Europe.   Live abroad as long as I live. The world may know we are separated, but they will know nothing more.   I do not reproach you for the great wrong I have suffered; perhaps I deserved it as a punishment for the many sins of my whole life—sins of pride, self-will, and ambition.   I did not love you; I knew you did not love me; and yet I stood at God's altar and accepted you as my husband.   All who have sinned as I have, surely have not received such complete and sudden chastisement as mine has been; but my sin may have been greater than that of others

who have acted similarly.   I could not plead sim-
plicity or want of understanding for my offence ;
I saw clearly that my views were all worldly—
all of pomp and vanity.   Had you been a more
worthy being than you were, my marrying you
must have ruined your peace; as it was, I was
only wrecked myself.

" I have just risen from a bed of great suffering ; but, thank God, I am spared from death
for a little while longer—yet a very little while.
Soon the world will be no more to me than if I
had never been born into it, yet I cannot altogether divest myself of the wish that my name
after death may not be uttered by the multitude
with solemn feelings of compassion for my great
misfortunes, and detestation of your enormity.
For this reason, and for the sake of my mother,
I will continue to bear publicly your name, and
the title it gives me; but I ask no more from you
—I can *claim* nothing.   Let all be allowed to

rest in silence from henceforth ; yet, oh ! I would entreat of you, in this my last communication, to think well over the past, and repent and turn from evil ways.   Avoid temptation, reform, and seek peace for your conscience.

"I am to leave Darktrees immediately with my dear friend, Miss Stutzer; we are going to Meiklam's Rest, having requested my cousin, Captain Crosbie, to permit us to spend some time there.   You and I must meet no more in this world ; but I shall expect to hear of the immediate sale of Darktrees, and all your property in the North of England.

" Elizabeth Pilmer."

*   *   *   *   *

Spring at Meiklam's Rest, with the flowers on the hills, and the violet perfumed breeze; with the birds building nests in sequestered bushes

and among the ivy in the house. Spring clothing
the woods with leaves—the old woods, where a
laughing, merry girl, and a joyous, spirited boy,
had played long years ago, shouting till the birds
fluttered from the branches, wondering at the
noise.   Spring everywhere; aye, in the heart of
London, where city tradesmen and weary-eyed ˙
milliners and dressmakers were busy and excited
with the bustle of " the season."   Spring and
life everywhere.   But no more was Lady Bend to
go to town—a sparkling belle amid the gay
throng that crowd west-end houses, when the
daisies and primroses begin to rear their heads in
lone spots in the country — no more to form
another unit among the multitudes of fluttering
gaudy creatures that crowd fashionable assem-
blies in the mighty world of London in " the
season ; " but to retire to the country, sobered,
saddened, willing to hide herself away from all
eyes.   A year ago, had not Lady Bend been the

most admired—the most beautiful young woman
in many ball-rooms?   Observe her now; a faded,
worn-looking being—no lustre in her eye—no
colour in her lips—the impress of a fearful
mental struggle stamped on every feature. She is
a wreck, indeed, yet bearing in her heart, amid the
storm and tempest of sorrow, a hope that never
raised its banner there before. Floating aloft,
above the ruins of battered, blackened strong-
holds of vanity and worldly pride, waves the
triumphant flag of victory—showing that a Conqueror has come to lay desolate the idols and
temples reared to false gods, and to build up
lasting monuments to Himself. Great wrestlings
are still going on in her soul—wrestlings between
the spirit and the flesh; and very desolating has
the warfare seemed, but a Hand is supporting her
through it all.

She was there at the lonely, quiet Rest, dreaming of old times, buried joys, buried friends. She

seemed all at once to have grown aged to a
remarkable extent; her hair was glistening more
and more with silver threads; her form atenu-
ated; yet, withal, she was lovely to behold.
Strangely beautiful seemed the moulding of her
features—the turn of her head—the grace of her
slender figure—the exquisite shape of hands and
feet.

Quiet as the Rest had been in former days, it
was still more quiet now; for Lady Bend chose
to have few servants, and to live in strict retirement.   Mrs. Pilmer was travelling abroad with
her daughter Mary, accompanied by a confidential
servant and a medical attendant; and they were
now far from England.   People at Yaxley and in
its neighbourhood knew that the baronet's wife
had come to Meiklam's Rest for the benefit of the
air there; they did not wonder where her husband was.   Perhaps she was a person too much
raised above the rank of the town gossips to be

the subject of as much comment as if she had been an equal, especially as she lived in solitude seeking no notice. She was evidently not in good health or spirits, and this fact saved her from envious observation.   The vicar, Mr. Hilbert, called upon her ; and the Ryders visited her; but after once returning their civilities, she was left unmolested by a repetition of them, except in the case of Mr. Hilbert, who now and then dropped in at the Rest to have a little talk with Miss Stutzer, whose past delinquencies were all forgotten since the discovery of Mrs. Meiklam's will, which had proved that she must have been in full favour since she grew up with the old lady, or else why receive a legacy of seven thousand pounds?   Mrs. Ryder, too, quite altered her opinion of Lizette, and invited her often to Yaxley; but the young girl never accepted the invitations.   She would not leave her friend alone, even if she had been inclined to seek companionship with Tom Ryder's sisters, which she was not.

Dillon Crosbie was all this time away on business, and also with his regiment at Chatham. He had never yet visited Yaxley since all that large property in its neighbourhood had come into his possession, but he corresponded frequently with his cousin at Meiklam's Rest. All that could give life to Lady Bend at this time were his letters, written full of life and hope—full of joyous aspirations. He was not dreaming of Bessie's sorrows ; he knew nothing of them—he would never know of them ; she was determined upon that. Her mother and Dillon !—oh, never, never, could she bear to break their hearts—hearts so fondly attached to her ! Neither would she confide her secret to her dear, devoted friend, Lizette Stutzer, to whom she owed so much. The secret concerned herself in all its mournful bearings. She was the sufferer. It was not necessary for *her* to confess it.

It was a lonely evening in June; the air, loaded with a thousand perfumes, was gently stirring odorous shrubs and gaudy tulips in the garden at Meiklam's Rest. Lady Bend was sitting on a rustic chair among the flowers; her friend had been reading to her, and they were both now silently looking upon the fair prospect before them. Dragon flies were darting through the little river that ran near, and the hum of bees, as they wandered round luscious flowers, sounded on the air. After a long pause Lady Bend spoke :—

" Lizette, it seems to me that I ought to employ myself in some way, and not remain as I am, wasting precious hours of life. Could I not, even here in retirement, make myself useful ?"

" Yes," replied Lizette, eagerly ; " and I think the exertion would do you good. We might establish a little school for poor children. Should you like teaching ?"

" I have never tried it since I used to give lessons to yourself," replied Bessie, sighing; "but I dare say I might be able to get on pretty well with it.   You know the people about here, Lizette, and you might collect such children as you think would most need our instruction; but they must come to the house at a certain hour each morning, and I will be ready to receive them."

" I think that would be a good arrangement, and you would feel the occupation most interesting after a time.   I shall see about it all to-morrow."

So Lizette hoped her dear friend was about to rouse herself from the miserable depression of spirits that had so long weighed her down, and she was glad to go among her old cottage friends round Yaxley, and ask them to send their children and grand-children to receive instruction from Lady Bend at Meiklam's Rest.   They all assented gratefully, and a little band of smiling-faced children was soon collected, who, in their neatest frocks, and with smoothly brushed hair, appeared at twelve o'clock on a bright summer morning, before the lady at the Rest—the beautiful wife of the great rich baronet, whose marriage the people in Yaxley and its neighbourhood had heard of with a sort of wondering awe. And yet how gently the great lady spoke; how sad her face looked, as if wealth and riches had not brought her such happiness as might have been expected.   How kindly she laid her hand on the sunny head of a golden-haired little one whose blue eyes were dancing joyously.   The sight of all these children seemed to unnerve the lady for a few minutes, and her voice trembled as she spoke to them—trembling because a chord of memory was touched, bringing back recollections of her own childhood's days.

" Shall we pray, Lizette?" she whispered almost timidly to her friend who was beside her.

" Yes, dear Bessie, let us open our meeting with a prayer and hymn," replied Lizette.

They were in the red room at the Rest, and there they all knelt down, while Lizette uttered a touching prayer, after which she asked some of the elder children to join in singing a little hymn which she herself had written for them when they attended her Sunday class long ago.

There was something most affecting to Lady Bend in the sound of so many wild little voices singing those simple words, and her tears flowed all the time ; but when the hymn was finished she grew calm, and entered with spirit into the new task she had undertaken. Gifted herself with a genius that had enabled her in childhood to learn like magic, she was, withal, more patient in giving instruction than many are who have themselves been slow in acquiring knowledge, and the work did not fatigue her. She taught the children Scripture, geography, and history, dividing them into classes, and, to Lizette's infinite thankfulness, seeming to forget her own sadness as she talked with each little girl, imparting her instructions with clearness and gentleness. When the youthful band was dismissed, Lady Bend said that she felt in better spirits than she had done for some months.

" I am glad, Lizette," she said, smiling, "that I have been able to do so much that was useful to-day. I do not feel quite so like a cumberer of the ground as I did before."

And so day by day her satisfaction increased, as she found her efforts to be of use succeeding, while her pupils spoke enthusiastically to their parents, round homely cottage hearths, of the

beautiful lady who never spoke crossly to them,
or frowned darkly when they made mistakes,
but went on patiently over again with a forgotten
lesson, to endeavour to make it clearer and more
impressive next time ; and they wished their
mothers could see her and hear her talk, for
though Miss Stutzer was pretty and gentle, too,
she was not like Lady Bend. They thought
Lady Bend was like a queen, and her condescension was more remarkable than that of Miss
Stutzer, who being one of the meek ones of the
earth, did not appear to have any natural inclina-
tions to strive against in her humility. But the
mothers had no chance of ever seeing the lady at
the Rest, for she never left the boundary of the
demesne even to take a carriage drive.

As the summer advanced, Lady Bend continued
her labours, and with pleasant smiles every morning welcomed her admiring little pupils, who
were rewarded according to their good behaviour,

and swift progress in learning, with beautiful presents – dolls dressed by her own hand, or books of useful information. Lizette for a little while hoped her dear friend would be restored to peace of mind and strength of body; but the hope gave way, when gradually she took note of the palpable wasting away of flesh, and the beam of a strange lustre in her eye—not like the lustre that had shone in it when she was a child, nor like the feverish light that had glowed in it often when she saw her at Markham; but another light, phosphorescent and peculiar, that warned of a coming enemy. Lizette felt that she was doomed to behold soon again the approach of the awful messenger that had so early revealed himself to her, even when she was a little child looking at her mother's corpse lying in its ghastly shroud, when her nurse told her God's messenger had called that mother from the world.

Time passed, and at length Lady Bend reclined

K 5

all day on the sofa, and spoke to her pupils without rising from it—teaching them from memory without the aid of books; and Lizette sent for Doctor Ryder, and he looked very stern when he looked at the faded form of the Baronet's wife, and he asked, in his abrupt way, where her husband was ; but Lady Bend only coloured faintly, and replied that Sir James was abroad.

" Humph ! then," muttered the doctor, " he ought to be here instead of anywhere else ;" and he felt the weak, irregular pulse, and looked again thoughtfully into the beaming, brilliant eyes, finally taking his leave with a thundercloud on his brow.

Time passed, and Lady Bend's voice was so faint that the children could only hear her speak when they bent near to her. They now regarded her with feelings of solemnity and awe, listening in deep, almost breathless silence to the words she spoke—words touching their immortal souls ; for their mothers had shaken their heads when they told how Lady Bend looked all white and pale like wax, with one little pink spot beaming on her cheek.

CHAPTER XX.

THE RETURN TO YAXLEY.

In September Mrs. Pilmer returned from her travels with Mary, who was still labouring under her unhappy malady, which rendered it necessary that she should be placed under the care of an eminent physician, who agreed to receive her in his private house for a handsome remuneration. From what Mrs. Pilmer knew herself of Sir James Bend's temper, she did not wonder that her daughter should wish to reside apart from him ; but she would have been much shocked at

the idea of a public separation ; her pride could
not have borne it.   Nothing of that sort was even
hinted at by Bessie—in fact, she never mentioned
her husband to either her mother or her cousin,
Dillon Crosbie.   The affairs of the latter were all
settled now ; his visits to Ireland on business and
his weary attendance in Dublin at law courts, were
all over.   He was now the undisputed possessor
of six thousand a-year, including Mrs. Meiklam's
legacy of the Meiklam's Rest property, and other
lands in the neigbourhood.   He met his aunt in
London on her return there with her unhappy
daughter Mary, and being anxious to see his
cousin, Lady Bend, and tell her how all his affairs
were settled, and perhaps anxious to see some one
else at the Rest also, he proposed to accompany
Mrs. Pilmer when she expressed her determination of going to see her daughter, Bessie, at
Yaxley.   Neither of them were aware of the
danger of Lady Bend's state.   They knew she

was living at the Rest for the benefit of the air
there, and that argued a certain degree of delicacy
of health ; but they knew nothing more.   In the
midst of all his bright hopes and plans —his
altered prospects —Dillon did not yet know of the
dusky cloud gathering over the apparently cloud-
less sky of his sudden prosperity   Well, indeed,
had Simon Peggs observed, there was "always a
dark spot somewhere, although everything may
seem fair and shining—a spot that tells us we
can't expect things to last perfect in this life ; we
must always be put in mind of the journey that's
coming to the other world for every one of us."

It was with very many mingled feelings that
Captain Crosbie entered Yaxley on the top of the
old coach that had borne him from it years ago,
when he was a wild boy, going to travel for the
first time on his own responsibility, to become a
pupil at a foreign school.   How vividly the past
all rushed back to him, as he beheld well-remem-

bered scenes ! There was the town looking nearly as it did of old, only, perhaps, the houses seeming to him shabbier and smaller than they did in days " lang syne." A thousand memories crowded to his mind—some very pleasant—some very sad. He saw the villa where his uncle had lived ; he saw the cottage where Mr. Stutzer had lived and died ; he saw the church spire rising solemnly above the graves where two dear friends were resting in their last earthly tenements. Ah, there were many changes in many things since he had last been at Yaxley ! He did not think of how much changed his own appearance was since those old days of boyhood, nor that many persons were watching eagerly to catch a glimpse of his figure as he jumped lightly down from the coach-roof at the hotel door. He had expressly charged his cousin not to make it publicly known that he was to arrive that evening, as he wished for no demonstrations of welcome on the part of those who were now his tenants; yet, somehow, the fact had gone abroad, faintly murmured here and there, till all the townspeople were on the *qui vive* to behold Mrs. Meiklam's heir. Many wondered and smiled—the women especially so, when they understood that the very elegant young man stepping down from the "Swift Hawk" was really Master Crosbie, the off-handed, sweet-tempered lad, who had always been a favourite, though by no means distinguished for elegance of dress or manner. Many old acquaint-ances came up to him touching their hats, and showing by broad grins how heartily they wel-comed him back to the neighbourhood, and he remembered them all quite well. When old Tom Fagg, the carpenter, asked him if he recol-lected the ship he had made for him when he was a little fellow not higher than his knee, the young man cheerily replied that he recollected it quite well, remarking that he had been in a great many

real ships since that time; and Tom thought the
young officer's smile did his heart good, and that
he was not one bit altered in kindliness since the
time he had begged his uncle, nearly twenty years
ago, to buy new tools for him in place of his old
ones, which were stolen from his humble work-
shop by a midnight thief.   And who was that
gray-haired, stooping man, hurrying over to shake
hands warmly with the hero of the evening,
eventually receiving such a hearty recognition
It was Mr. Benson, Crosbie's old schoolmaster,
altering and ageing with the advance of years,
but bearing freshly in his mind the memory of
that most noble-minded of pupils.   We must
recognise at once the next figure that approached
the young man—the wrinkled, wild-eyed, crazed
creature, who drew near to him, holding out her
withered hand, dark and sinewy, to receive the
friendly grasp accorded to it.

" I am glad to see you, Jenny," he said kindly.

"You must come up to the Rest, that we may have a talk together."

"Ay, sir, I'll go there. I have a duty to perform at the Rest; I want to see Lady Bend; I haven't seen her since she came to the neighbourhood; I was loath to intrude upon her."

"Come then, and see me, too," said Captain Crosbie, slipping a sovereign into her hand, not with any parade of patronage and condescension, but just with the same frank kindliness with which he had often drawn a sixpence from his waistcoat pocket for the old woman in his boyish days. Yes, Tom Fagg was right; he was not one bit altered since early youth; he had known how to bear his dependence bravely and cheerfully, and now he knew equally well how to bear his riches and prosperity humbly and steadily. He had never been abject or cast down; he would never be haughty or overbearing.

But Mrs. Pilmer could not be kept waiting in

the dingy little parlour of the hotel while her nephew talked to old friends. He had to hurry from sincere congratulations and humble welcomes, and join her with alacrity; for, though she owed him now thousands of pounds, he was just as attentive to her as when she was the creditor, he the debtor. He handed her into the carriage waiting for them at the inn, and they were soon driving quickly to Meiklam's Rest. Dillon was thoughtful all the way, scarcely speaking to his aunt, who was filled with happiness at the thoughts of meeting the only being she had ever loved ardently in her life. Dillon was dwelling upon how he would see Lady Bend, brightly smiling as he narrated many amusing adventures to her. He thought she must surely by this time have recovered from her first grief and shock about her sister, which had apparently upset her so much at Darktrees, and she would

be able to laugh over his anecdotes, as in former
days.   She would be pleased to hear what simple-
minded, good-natured people his Irish tenants
were, and how they were all pleased to welcome
him for their landlord, as a descendant of the
hospitable old Crosbie family, the members of
which, among their many faults, had never been
accused of anything like unkindness or tyranny.
It had amused Dillon when old women in red
cloaks, and with unbonneted heads, and old men
in strangely fashioned long coats with enormous
capes, had all agreed, on beholding him on his
new estates in Connaught, that he was "the
very moral and pattern of the ould Colonel, his
grandfather, and he was the handsomest man to
be seen in the biggest fair in Ireland, and that
was a big word."   And we will not say that
Master Crosbie did not feel flattered at the com-
pliment, nor that he did not consider it to be

pretty well deserved too, for he had not passed
the age of twenty-five without finding out that
he was something beyond the common as to appearance.   There were many kind friends to tell
him that he was decidedly "the best-looking
fellow" in his regiment, and nearly always the
handsomest man quartered in any garrison.   But
he only regarded this knowledge as a matter of
fact, of an agreeable enough description, but not
sufficiently astounding to unsettle his wits.
Nevertheless he fully intended to laugh with
Bessie over the compliments paid him by his
Irish friends.   Yet let not the reader imagine that
Captain Crosbie had no other thoughts connected with the inhabitants of Meiklam's Rest;
he had some feelings buried very deep in his
heart, which rose and fell often at the recollec-
tion of one fair being dwelling within those walls
that he was fast approaching.   The carriage

drove up the well-remembered avenue, where the
fine old trees were changing their colour from the
green of summer to the copper hues of autumn,
the air was still, the birds twittering out some of
their final songs, before winging their flight to
distant climes. The summer had been very
lovely, and was lingering longer than usual.
Nothing but the colour of the trees, and the fast-
falling twilight could have told that it was so
near autumn.

Now the house was reached. Dillon's heart
began to beat violently; not with emotion, because he was looking at the old mansion that he
could now call his own ; not because all those
lands, stretching far away, so beautifully planned
and wooded, were in his possession, but from a
feeling that he was about to meet one dearer to
him than houses or lands or any earthly treasure.
The door-bell has been rung.   Mrs.   Pilmer

wonders that her dear child is not out on the steps watching for her. She does not know, perhaps, that she has arrived, perhaps not. Dillon's cheek is very pale, as he enters the wide, old-fashioned hall.

CHAPTER XXI.

THE MEETING—THE BLESSING.

LIZETTE STUTZER's hand was soon clasped most fervently in his; she had met the new comers in the hall. Bessie was not there. Where was she?

"In the red room," replied Lizette, who was not aware of how lightly Bessie had written of her own illness to her friends. "She is on the sofa there."

"Ah, lazy girl!" exclaimed Mrs. Pilmer, "I am afraid she is going to treat us to some fine lady airs and conceits. This would not have been the way she would have welcomed her mother before, she was married; would it, Dillon?"

This was said playfully, for the lady was in a wondrous gracious humour. Lizette was not attending to her words, for Captain Crosbie had been whispering some sentences to her that rather scattered her thoughts for the moment.

And now they all went to the red room, Lizette leading the way in silence. They stood within it.

" My God!"

That was the exclamation of the mother when she beheld her child; it was uttered involuntarily, impulsively—in surprise—in alarm. The changed wasted form scared her.

" My dear Bessie!" said Dillon, embracing her ardently.

Then there was a silence.   Mrs. Pilmer hastily left the room.   Dillon felt unable to utter a sentence for a long while.   Lady Bend well knew why her mother had quitted her so abruptly, and why her cousin's heart seemed damped so palpably; and she almost regretted that she had not prepared them to find her as she was, too weak to walk across the room without support. She was the first to speak cheerfully herself, and when the agitation of meeting her friends had passed off, she talked happily all the evening. Mrs. Pilmer, by a mighty effort, strove to conceal her alarm and grief; she was glad Sir James was abroad, for otherwise she would not have ventured near her daughter; therefore she made no comments upon his conduct in thus abandoning his wife in her precarious state of health; but Dillon thought he was behaving barbarously. Could his neglect and cruelty be breaking his wife's heart?   Oh, what a dark thought!   Had he known the truth, how much darker it would have been!

No more did the cousins walk together, as of old, through the woods of Meiklam's Rest; nevermore would they visit, hand in hand, or arm in arm, the haunts of happy childhood; yet Bessie had learned at last the full meaning and import of the "peace that passeth understanding." The storm was over; now there was a calm—all tempest hushed. Her daily exercise consisted now in her feeble walk, supported by Lizette and her mother, from her chamber to the red room, and from the red room to her chamber; what she heard and saw of outward sounds and scenes was from the open window where her sofa was occasionally wheeled, and the song of birds, and the breath of breezes, came wafted in, and she looked out upon the spreading woods where her footsteps would be known no more. Cheerfully she talked to her Cousin Dillon, and cheerfully he tried to answer her; but her tones sounded to him more like the far off ringing of a funeral bell, wafted musically on the wind, than the speech of human voice. For a long while Captain Crosbie did not speak of a hope that was very near his heart, either to the object of it, or to his cousin; he seemed to have forgotten self and selfish feeling altogether, but Bessie spoke on the subject herself, telling him that it was her earnest wish that he should try and win the love of her friend Lizette.

"You have always been most dear to me, my cousin," she said, speaking tremulously, "and I am convinced that your happiness in every way would be secured by a marriage with that most excellent of beings. Dillon, she is worthy of you, and you are worthy of her."

"I wish I could think I was," replied Dillon, thoughtfully.

Bessie checked the enthusiastic exclamation

that arose to her lips, and remained silent for a little time; but her heart was beating almost audibly.

Just then some altercation sounded from below in the hall, and on requesting to know what it arose from, Lady Bend was informed that the crazy fortune-teller, Jenny Black, was wishing to come up and see her.

" Let her come," said the lady, gently.

And so she appeared within the red room, her face and hands cleaner than usual, and a fantastic bonnet shielding her matted locks from observation. She had dressed herself with care before venturing to demand an interview with the great lady.

" I came here this day to bless you, Miss Bessie," she said abruptly, when the first salutations were over and she had wrung the small, slight hand of Lady Bend mournfully enough. " You remember I cursed you once, and now I'm

going to give you my blessing.   Long ago I had
a dream; it was in the summer time, and the
hay was cutting in the fields, and I chose to
sleep that night away out among the sweet grass
of the meadows, all dry and crisp round me.   I
chose to stay there, you see, because it's out in
the night that spirits descend and whisper to you
the things that are coming to pass.   So, Miss
Bessie, I slept, and I dreamed that you stood
before me, worn and fleshless, nothing but a
skeleton, and your hair had grown white, and yet
you looked young in the face; and says you,
'Jenny, you cursed me long ago, and see now
what I've come to.   I'm blighted sore indeed,
and my heart's broken, and my health's gone,
and I'm come here to die at Meiklam's Rest; but
you must bless me before I die, and pray for me.'
There was more that you told me, too, but says
you, 'Jenny, you mustn't ever tell mortal being
what *that* was.   On the day of judgment all will

be known.' So I won't speak of it here, before Captain Crosbie and Miss Lizette."

The singular agitation that the old woman's words produced in Lady Bend, passed for the natural nervousness of her delicate health in the eyes of Dillon and Lizette, who were both present. They wished to persuade Jenny to leave the room, but Bessie preferred to let her remain. Raising her withered hands upwards, the old woman closed her eyes and pronounced solemnly these words, standing beside the sofa where Bessie was re-clining :—

" I bless you here this day ; I pray that you may have peace outwardly and inwardly ; that all grief and pain may pass away ; that your Father in Heaven may take you to Himself."

" Thank you, Jenny," said the lady, extending her hand to her once more, " forgive me for all my hasty words in old times ; we are good friends now."

Jenny said nothing ; grim her face looked ; no tear was in her eye, yet she was murmuring all the way back to the hall-door, and all the way down the avenue, and all the way through tangled copses and glens.

" Oh, poor thing !—poor thing ! Withered and worn indeed; she going and I staying behind ; she with gold and servants, and food and fire— everything in plenty and to spare—dying there, more heartbroken, more humbled than Crazy Jenny—half naked, obliged to eat the husks and the castaways, and gather brambles for the winter's fire ! Oh, poor thing !—poor thing !"

CHAPTER XXII.

NO MORE.

In the midst of a great sorrow, Lizette had two bright consolations. The first was, that her beloved friend, Bessie, had laid fast hold of the Christian's hope and stay; the second that she was herself the affianced wife of one who had long been dear to her.   Dillon Crosbie had sought and won; she was now his promised bride, and never did trusting heart feel more perfectly sure that

L 5

its happiness was safe in the keeping it had been resigned to than hers did, when she gave it confidingly to him. Bessie was glad when they told her they were betrothed, and with her own pale hands she joined theirs together, saying she felt quite sure that they were perfectly suited for each other.

We shall not linger over the final struggle of that sad parting between the spirit and the flesh. Very sad, indeed, it was. The messenger seemed to come and go with almost tantalizing uncertainty, and then he came really when no one was looking for him. Bessie died in the red room of the Rest, lying on her sofa, near the window, when the autumn sun was just setting in a red light that glowed upon the hills and valleys for a few minutes, and then vanished to rest like a departed soul. She had just been calling attention to the lines of the poet—

"Sweet sabbath of the year,
    While evening lights decay,
Thy parting steps methinks I hear,
    Steal from the world away.
Amid thy silent bowers,
    'Tis sad but sweet to dwell,
Where falling leaves and drooping flowers,
    Around me breathe farewell"—

when her spirit passed away—peacefully, as if her eyes were only closed in slumber. Bessie's face wore a look of great and holy composure. Life had departed like a bird flying from an open cage. The strife was indeed over for her; but woe to the mother left behind. That grief was unutterable—indescribable. Night and day sorrowing; night and day—when the stars kept watch on high, and the sunlight gleamed afar. Yet, oh, woman! when you beheld the numberless, spangling worlds dotting the winter skies, why not have thought that your beloved one was now beholding face to face the Creator of the universe? Why, when weeping so bitterly at the music of the choir in the simple church at Yaxley, hymning out praises to the Eternal, did you not remember that the departed one was standing round the throne, joining in the song of Moses and the Lamb?

According to Bessie's request, confided to Dillon and Lizette, her remains were buried in the vault of the Meiklam family in the churchyard at Yaxley.

" Not with your husband's family, dear Bessie?" Dillon had said when she uttered the wish.

" I wish to be buried with my dear friend, Mrs. Meiklam," was the faint reply.

And so, most faithfully, as though it were a sacred duty, her cousin fulfilled every little request mentioned to him. Her husband was away in Egypt or New Zealand, nobody exactly knew where; but they knew he did not attend his wife's funeral. Sad and solemn funeral. The burial of a young person cut off in the bloom and beauty of youth is always a solemn ceremony. Dillon

Crosbie was chief mourner—chief and sincerest of mourners, indeed.   According to the wish of the mothers of those children whom Lady Bend had continued to instruct up to the last moment that strength was spared her, they were all present at the funeral—a youthful band of sorrowing little ones, all clad in white, forming a touching group that moved all hearts.   They sang a hymn round the coffin before it was lowered into its resting place, where it was to remain till earth and sea were called upon to surrender their dead ; and when the last notes of their voices had died upon the air, the coffin was borne into the dim vault—vanishing from the eyes of the chief mourner, who stood as in a trance, with a confused rush of thought surging through his brain.   Gone for ever from human sight, that most lovely of human forms ; silent for ever to mortal ears, that silvery, pleasant voice !

" Patience, oh, my soul, patience," he murmured ; yet he stood there bewildered very long, with the sighing of the wind sounding in his ears, as it rustled through the long grass of the churchyard. A hand gently touched his arm, it was that of Dr. Ryder, who with great tears standing in his own eyes, drew him away com- passionately.

*   *   *   *   *

For a long while a dark shadow rested over the house of Meiklam's Rest. Mrs. Pilmer wished to remain there in her anguish ; and Lizette stayed with her. Sir James Bend's movements were unknown to any of Bessie's friends. He was nothing to them now. Was he relieved when he heard of that long-wished for death, which at the request of the dying one was never announced in the public papers ? His own heart knew. Dark- trees Hall was sold; the town-house in Park-lane was disposed of; he went abroad, and was lost to his old acquaintances.

One dim winter evening, Lizette and Dillon Crosbie were sitting alone together in the red room of the Rest. The former was looking over an album of her deceased friend, containing various little scraps of her own writing, and some pieces of verse. There were some lines, signed with her own name, which struck Lizette, and she read them out for Dillon. It was headed thus :—

MY EARLY LOVE.

"I thought of thee when the spring sent forth
  Fresh grass and sweet wild flowers,
And the green leaves gave their shelter out
  To form the young year's bowers.
And my thought of thee resembled then
  The breath of the fragrant breeze,
That wafted o'er meadows cool and green,
  And soft through the new clad trees.

" I thought of thee in the summer time,
  When the sun sent forth its heat,
To ripen the orchard's rosy fruit,
  And the golden ears of wheat.
And my thought of thee was like the glow
  Of the warmth that parched the land ;
It beamed as the Eastern sunshine beams
  On desert plains of sand.

"I thought of thee when the autumn wind
  Howled wildly o'er hill and vale,
And russet leaves were carried away
  On the breath of the moaning gale.
And my thought of thee grew wilder then,
  As wild as the rushing blast,
That seemed to tell with every breath
  Of dead hopes drifting past.

"And now I think in the dim nights long,
  When the stars shed out no glow,
And o'er rock and hill, and deep dark sea,
  The winter fog hangs low.
And sad, oh, sad ! is my thought of thee,
  As I ponder o'er and o'er,
On the many seasons lost in the shade,
  Of a past that returns no more !"

"Whom could she thus have loved?" asked Lizette, wonderingly, as she finished reading the verses.

"Most probable it was a fancy sketch," said Dillon, looking thoughtfully from the window at the wintry view outside. The old trees were standing with a desolate aspect, bare and gaunt, upwards towards the leaden sky.

"A fancy sketch, you think?" said Lizette raising her eyes, and fixing them for a second or

two on her companion's face. She thought Dillon
had made a mistake in that suggestion, and she
was right.   Bessie had written no fancy sketch ;
but her cousin had never discovered the object of
her early love ; he never dreamed that an early
love existed at all, for it was a love that Bessie
concealed very successfully.   The object of it was
poor in worldly riches ; and trained, as she had
been from childhood, to consider wealth and
rank precious above all things, she no more
dreamed of ever uniting her fate with his than he
dreamed of asking her, and so the secret lay buried
with others in the grave, leaving Dillon and
Lizette to puzzle it out as they best might.
Perhaps the latter was more clear sighted on the
subject than her betrothed husband was.   Her
suspicions hovered very near the truth, but Dillon
not being able to call to memory (such a fine long
memory as he had, too), any early friend of his
cousin who was at all worthy of her love, or likely

to inspire it, he gave the matter up as an impene-
trable mystery.   Very much astonished, indeed,
he would have been had any one whispered to him
the name of him, who for so many years had been
the unconscious possessor of her whole heart; but
had any one whispered it to Lizette, she would not
have been in the least surprised.

CHAPTER XXIII.

A GREAT BUSTLE IN YAXLEY AND ITS

NEIGHBOURHOOD.

Mrs. Bromley began to get somewhat annoyed that her niece did not choose to return to Lone-hill, and she consequently had several violent outbursts of passion with her servants and Simon Peggs, and Martin Hicks got warning seven times in as many months to quit her service. But things all came right when Lizette wrote to her that she was only waiting for her consent and

approval of her choice to become the wife of one
worthy of all honour and love, who had sought her
hand ; and when Mrs. Bromley understood that
this estimable young man had six thousand a-year,
and was, moreover, descended from a fine old
family, she gave her full consent and hearty congratulations.   The old lady was anxious that the
wedding should take place under her own auspices
at Lonehill, where she told Lizette she would
arrange everything tastefully and handsomely for
the ceremony ; she would get the rooms papered,
and swept out, and the carpets shaken ; she would
have her handsome chairs polished brightly, and
the parlour fitted up for the *dejeuner* in great style.
Yet, Lizette could not be persuaded by these
tremendous inducements to give up her own and
her lover's wish of being married at Yaxley.   Mrs.
Pilmer was still at Meiklam's Rest, and she
kindly took an interest in her nephew's approach-

ing marriage. The two young people about to be united were becoming dear to her, for the sake of one who had loved them so well, and she promised to superintend the wedding arrangements, though she would not consent to appear among the guests. Mrs. Bromley being invited to Yaxley, arrived there in due course of time, very stately and grand, attired in some costly dress that had been taken from its abiding place in a trunk at Lonehill, and which, though somewhat old-fashioned in material and shaping, still lent a certain dignity to her tall figure. She behaved with much propriety at the Rest, and was satisfied that Captain Crosbie was gentlemanly and handsome. She whispered to Lizette that she was sure he would never have married her if he knew what a mean little fellow her father was, and the young lady only smiled, without saying anything. The wedding morning came—

—— " Light stole upon the clouds
With a strange beauty.   Earth received again
Its garment of a thousand dyes ; and leaves,
And delicate blossoms, and the painted flowers,
And everything that bendeth to the dew,
And stirreth with the daylight, lifted up
Its beauty to the breath of that sweet morn."

It was a bright spring morning, when the sun glittered on young green leaves and fresh dewy meadows.   Since break of day the song of birds had ascended from brake, and dell and shady grove, making the woods resound with tuneful carols.   Violets from sequestered spots, and every wild flower from hill and vale had early sent tributes of perfume to the air.   Nature seemed to have proclaimed a holiday.   The breeze no longer busy, wandered leisurely among the verdant trees, breathing lightly as it passed; the fields lay peacefully basking in the yellow sunshine ; the trees, the hedges, the hills appeared as if clothed in gala dresses, for the glorious light of the spring day made all things fair and brilliant to the eye.   But fair as inanimate nature looked, fairer still was the lovely bride who stood that day in the church of Yaxley before the altar, with her bride-groom at her side, exchanging vows only to be dissolved by death. Sweet to both was the bondage they were voluntarily sealing there. Though shadowed by a dreamy pensiveness, the bride's features wore an expression of holy calm and trust that thought of earthly happiness could not alone have imparted. Young as she was, she had drunk deeply of the world's sorrows, and she knew that the earthly pilgrimage of man was beset by many cares. Yet fearlessly she looked into the future—fearlessly as a child clinging to its father's hand, while it leads her through an unknown country.

Lizette's bridesmaids were the Miss Ryders, who had themselves offered to attend her in that capacity. Their brother Tom—though happening to be about that time at Yaxley for a short visit

—preferred setting off at once for London, to making his appearance at the wedding, when he was not to play a very principal part in the ceremony. His sisters could not imagine why Tom was so capricious and extraordinary. His mother never knew that her dear son, Tom—her handsome, fine-looking boy, the pet and treasure of her heart, who was too good for anybody— had been refused by a poor, penniless girl, who at that time had no home, no money, no one to protect her. Ah, no! Mrs. Ryder, you did not know *that*, though you had often asked Tom, latterly, why he had not thought of proposing for Miss Stutzer, now when she was here in the neighbourhood; and Tom had always hastily left the room at that question, never answering it.

" How men forget their old loves," Mrs. Ryder had observed one day to her daughters. " There is Tom that never speaks a word of Lizette Stutzer now, and seems quite annoyed if I want

him to go to Meiklam's Rest, and see her! Well,
well! It's only women that have lasting feelings
in this way. I suppose he has fallen in love
with some new girl in town, or maybe he has
found out that it is better to remain single."

The day before the wedding Tom started for
London, and was in the great busy city in his
dusty office in Thames-street, where the sun
never shone very brightly at any time of the
year, on the day that Lizette became the wife of
his old school rival, Dillon Crosbie. We cannot
precisely say what the reason of it was, but Tom's
eyes were very red that morning. Perhaps he
had caught cold travelling the day before; perhaps he had been reading too much lately;
perhaps he had been weeping. None knew but
himself as he sat there, at his dingy desk, writing
—writing all the day—fancying often he heard a
merry church peal ringing in his ears—the echo
of the bell sounding forth its summons and its

welcome from the homely church at Yaxley. Oh, world of joy and sorrow! Some rejoicing—some suffering—marriage peals and funeral bells ringing together—the wedding and the burial coming alternately! Hope rising and sinking as the ebb and flow of the tide.

The ceremony was over—the ring upon the bride's fairy finger, and there she was leaving the church leaning on her husband's arm, with the girls of her Sunday-school class, in gay dresses, strewing flowers on her path as she walked to her carriage. But what was this? The horses were taken from the carriage, and many stout young tenants of Captain Crosbie were waiting there to draw it from the church to Meiklam's Rest, where the *déjeuner* was prepared. Oh, yes; all honour must be done to the nuptials of that most honourable of landlords. The breakfast at the Rest was quite superb. Even Mrs. Bromley, who was very exacting as regarded the arrangements of other people, pronounced each appointment to be quite *comme il faut.* Very stately and grand did the old lady appear among the guests. Everything went off well. Dillon Crosbie's groomsman was a brother officer and particular friend from the depôt, who made himself remarkably agreeable to the bridesmaids— to one of whom he seemed to have taken a fancy; and there was some flirting, and soft speeches, and well-timed allusions. The large bridecake, with its strange and elaborate ornaments, was all cut away to provide the young ladies with pieces to dream upon, and to send to their friends for a similar purpose; and we sincerely hope it was more efficacious in producing appropriate dreams than any bridecake we have ever slept on, reader. Ah, such dreamless nights as those were, passed with a tiny piece of rich cake, stuck over with the nine pins requisite to complete the charm, under our pillow!

The company at length dispersed. The coach, new and sparkling, with its four fine horses proudly holding their heads on high, waited at the door for the bride and bridegroom; and, amid the congratulations of humble but faithful friends, the really happy pair were swiftly borne on their way to London. Past the cottages, where white-haired men and women stood smiling and murmuring blessings, the carriage rolled along; past the churchyard where the silent dead were lying; past the cottage where Paul Stutzer had sat upon a lonely winter night, many years ago, despairing because he thought his child might yet be a workhouse pauper; past the large schoohouse, where merry boys, who had heard, as of beautiful legends handed down from generation to generation, stories of the noble and heroic deeds performed by the noble boy who years ago had studied in that schoolroom, and played in that playground, huzzaed heartily, waving their caps on high.   Cheers were heard on all sides as the vehicle passed through the little town; and hats were lifted from many heads, both of old and young, to testify respect for the bride and bridegroom passing by ; for as children they had been loved, and now they were loved and honoured in YAXLEY AND ITS NEIGHBOURHOOD.

THE END.

T. C. NEWBY, 30, Welbeck Street, Cavendish Square, London.

M 3

FAMILY MOURNING.

MESSRS. JAY

Would respectfully announce that great saving may be made by
purchasing Mourning at their Establishment,

THEIR STOCK OF

FAMILY MOURNING

BEING

THE LARGEST IN EUROPE.

MOURNING COSTUME

OF EVERY DESCRIPTION

KEPT READY-MADE,

And can be forwarded to Town or Country at a moment's notice.

The most reasonable Prices are charged, and the wear of every
Article Guaranteed.

THE LONDON

GENERAL MOURNING WAREHOUSE,

247 & 248, REGENT STREET,

(NEXT THE CIRCUS.)

JAY'S.

EMULATION, in whatever pursuit, where general utility is the object in view, is one of the immutable privileges of Genius; but it requires no slight degree of perspicuous attention to distinguish Originality from Imitation, and the exercise of Caution becomes of more than usual importance, where the effect of a remedial application (both as regards health and personal appearance), is the subject of consideration; these observations are imperatively called for from A. ROWLAND & SONS, of London, whose successful introduction of several articles of acknowledged and standard excellence for the Toilet has given rise to fertility of imitation, perfectly unprecedented; they would have deemed observation unnecessary were temporary deceptions unaccompanied by permanently injurious effects—it is with reference to ROWLANDS' KALYDOR *for the Complexion*, that the Public are particularly interested in the present remarks. This preparation eminently *balsamic, restorative,* and *invigorating;*—the result of scientific botanical research, and equally celebrated for safety in application, as for unfailing efficacy in *removing all Impurities and Discolorations of the Skin*, has its "Spurious Imitations of the most deleterious character," containing mineral astringents utterly ruinous to the Complexion, and, by their repellant action endangering health, which render it indispensably necessary to see that the words " ROWLANDS' KALYDOR" are on the wrapper, with the signature in red ink, "*A. Rowland & Sons.*" Sold by Chemists and Perfumers.

In Three Vols. 31s. 6d.

A RIGHT-MINDED WOMAN.

A Novel.

By FRANK TROLLOPE.

In 2 vols.,

KATE KENNEDY.

A Novel.

By the Author of " Wondrous Strange."

www.ingramcontent.com/pod-product-compliance
Lightning Source LLC
Chambersburg PA
CBHW030802020726
47499CB00006B/1731